Panda Books
The Scholar and the Serving Maid

The writer Fang Ai, born in 1928 in Fenghua, Zhejiang Province, is president of the Shanghai Research Institute of Film and Television Literature. He began writing and publishing poems and dramas in 1949 when he wrote for a People's Liberation Army drama group.

In the sixties he became a high school teacher but continued writing in his spare time. His play *Recover the Lost Ground* was staged all over the country in the early seventies and was made into a film.

In the early eighties, he joined the Shanghai Television Station as a playwright. He and his team wrote the scripts for several TV serials including *Tidal Wave; Oriental Hotel* and *The Scholar and the Serving Maid*. Later, he adapted the TV script into a novel. He also edited the scripts of the TV serials *Monk Ji* and *Morning in Shanghai*, which enjoyed large audiences. A number of his film scripts has been filmed by the Shanghai Film Studio and Guangxi Film Studio.

Fang Ai

The Scholar and the Serving Maid

(A Qing Dynasty Mystery)

Translated by Yu Fanqin
and Esther Samson

Panda Books

Panda Books
First Edition 1994
Copyright 1994 by CHINESE LITERATURE PRESS
ISBN 7−5071−0224−6 / I . 221
ISBN 0−8351−3141−6

Published by CHINESE LITERATURE PRESS
Beijing 100037, China
Distributed by China International Book Trading Corporation
35 Chegongzhuang Xilu, Beijing 100044, China
P.O. Box 399, Beijing, China
Printed in the People's Republic of China

CONTENTS

Preface	7
Goat Eating Cabbage	9
Forced into A Liaison	25
Slaughter A Goat and Frame It	39
Murder the Husband to Get the Wife	50
Place One Man's Blame on Another	61
The Goat Falls into Tiger Jaws	74
A Sinister Hand Blocks the Sky	85
No Reverse of Verdict	97
Re-examination in Hangzhou	107
Knots and Twists	116
Officials Cover Up for Officials	128
A Long Dark Night	137

Singing and Tears	141
An Unexpected Breakthrough	147
Shedding Blood in the Yamen	153
To Lodge A Petition in the Capital	165
Prodding the Prince with Wit	171
Lying on A Board of Spikes	181
Taking the Prisoners to the Capital	191
Lifelong Affinity	202
Epilogue	208

Preface

THIS is a true story about love and murder. It was one of four famous cases which took place during the Qing Dynasty (1644 – 1911). This particular case concerned two young sweethearts and was tried by over a hundred officials from county level upwards until it reached the ears of the Empress Dowager herself.

People claimed that the Empress Dowager Cixi never did a single good thing during her reign, but she did intervene to clear the two young people accused of murder — the scholar Yang Naiwu and the maid Bi Xiugu — and removed the corrupt officials involved in the case from their posts. But the feudal attitudes of the time still kept the two young lovers apart for life.

Before writing the book, the author, Fang Ai, read through all the case files of the Qing Dynasty Board of Punishments, now stored in the No. One National Archives. He also read the newspaper reports of the case, and an article by Naiwu's daughter. The great-great-grandson of Naiwu also cooperated in providing extra material so that the author was able to tell this poignant story against a background of Qing Dynasty corruption.

Goat Eating Cabbage

THIS is not fiction, but a true account of what happened to two innocent young people which aroused the sympathy and indignation of people ever since it happened over 100 years ago.

On Pagoda Hill outside the county town of Yuhang lies the beautiful West Lake. Two pagodas — one representing a man, the other a woman — soar into the sky. A clear stream, spanned by the Stone Lion Bridge, flows through the town.

A girl in her late teens, a charming beauty with fair regular features, descended the stone steps leading to the stream and rinsed a basket of green cabbages.

A country urchin, hiding behind a willow tree, threw a stone into the stream, splashing water over the girl's face. She showed no sign of anger or reaction, but meekly wiped her face with the corner of her apron as if she was used to abuse and ill-treatment.

Emboldened by the lack of response, the urchin sang in a mocking voice:

Little Cabbage, oh Little Cabbage,
You have neither dad nor mum.
As a childbride, your suffering is too deep to tell,
You cry your heart out late at night.

She lowered her head and saw her reflection in the water; a head of beautiful black hair, a face fair and young, with big eyes under arched eyebrows. Her mouth was like a small red cherry under a well-shaped nose. She wore her favourite outfit, a green blouse and trousers with a white apron tied round her waist. She looked as fresh and tender as a green cabbage and neighbours soon forgot her real name of Bi Xiugu and called her Little Cabbage* instead.

Suddenly a robust young man appeared and pushed the urchin aside. "Shut your dirty mouth!" he shouted.

"I was only singing," the boy whined, "and anyway what's it got to do with you?"

"You shouldn't sing such songs," the young man replied.

As the boy scampered away, he shouted: "You're hen-pecked even before you're married to her."

Little Cabbage appeared blind and deaf to the incident and even to the spring-like surroundings about her. She mounted the steps with her basket of washed vegetables and walked away.

When Nanjing fell to the Qing troops, she and her parents fled north. Unfortunately, her mother got lost on the way. She and her father made it to Yuhang where they settled down. When she was seven years old, her father, who had been a teacher, died of illness during the Taiping Rebellion. She was sold as a childbride so that she could have money to bury her father. Her betrothed was an apprentice bean-curd maker and his widowed mother worked as a maid in

---

*Here referring to a slender-looking Chinese cabbage, whose upper half is green and lower half white.

the house of the scholar Yang Naiwu.

Yang Naiwu was in his late twenties and had passed the first of the imperial examinations at county level. His parents had also died when he was a boy and he was brought up by his elder sister, Shuying, a widow with a young son. He was a pleasant, cultured man, and had a strong sense of justice, particularly when it came to defending the weak against the powerful. Well-versed in medical matters, he often gave his services, free, to those who could not afford to pay.

He was in his study one day reading a book when his sister walked in with Little Cabbage.

"Servant Ge is ill, brother, so she has sent her future daughter-in-law Xiugu to do the cleaning."

She looked at the nervous girl who stood with lowered head, and added: "I think she can do the laundry and get you tea. In the meantime pop over to Mrs. Ge and see how she is."

So Naiwu rushed to the Ges. He felt Mrs. Ge's pulse and wrote out a prescription.

Little Cabbage had never met anyone so kind and considerate before. As Naiwu handed her the prescription for Mrs. Ge, their eyes met and she blushed. He felt something stir within his breast as he saw her with different eyes. "No wonder people say that the childbride of the Ges' is called Little Cabbage, but no cabbage is as pretty or as pure as she is..." His admiring glances made her bold and she coquettishly offered him tea and a seat.

Xiugu was happy to take over the cleaning work and as she dusted the books and writing brushes in the study, she remembered how her father guided her stubby fingers as she held the brush to write characters when she was six years old. Her eyes filled with tears.

She did not hear Naiwu's footsteps as he entered the room, but came to with a start when he called her name softly: "Xiugu!" Embarrassed for having forgotten herself, she said: "Master," and quickly replaced the brush and left the room.

What emotions were stirring in his breast! He walked over to the fish bowl and watched the slow-moving black and red goldfish and then started to paint.

Xiugu returned with tea and stood quietly behind the absorbed Naiwu. He seemed to be able to endow the ordinary brush in his hand with a magic power and soon two lifelike goldfish appeared on the paper.

"That's marvellous!" Xiugu exclaimed out loud.

"Do you like painting?" he asked.

"Yes," she replied.

"Well, why not have a try?"

He held her hand as she tentatively dipped the brush in the ink and swished it on the paper. In a few strokes, they had outlined a juicy tender little cabbage.

Xiugu blushed furiously and dropped the brush.

"I have been taking special notice of the cabbages in the fields these days and I realized little cabbages, green, delicate and natural, far surpass gorgeous peonies."

A slight smile appeared on her face which made him more daring.

"You are bright. If you like, I can teach you how to paint."

Xiugu's eyes lit up but just as suddenly she became

downcast.

"I am much too lowly to rise above my station," she said.

"But your father was a teacher. Were it not for the war, you would have become a young mistress. You're intelligent. I want to teach you."

"Really?" the surprised Xiugu asked with pleasure. Naiwu nodded.

Another morning. An early morning with a sky of rosy clouds.

Xiugu was walking slowly beside the clear stream with a basket of freshly washed clothes. This was the first time since she had become a childbride that she felt in high spirits. She saw with new eyes the beauty of the fields, and felt the advent of spring stirring within her. On Pagoda Hill the male and female pagodas soared into the sky. Before her was the Stone Lion Bridge over the stream which was so clear that the scales of fish glittered through dappled water. The weeping willows swayed, peach trees were in full blossom, and brightly-coloured butterflies darted about searching for mates. Xiugu picked a spray of peach blossom and then as if recalling something, her face reddened and she shook her head slightly. She looked down as she climbed up the stone bridge and at first did not notice two pairs of men's shoes blocking her way. She moved aside to continue but the satin shoes also moved and she was forced to look up to see two young men, dressed in expensive clothes, standing before her. Their eyes darted from her face to her body and she lowered her eyes in embarrassment.

They were two n'er-do-wells. One was Qian

Baosheng, owner of the Benevolent Pharmacy; the other was Liu Zihe, the son of the newly-appointed county magistrate. Baosheng was a beady-eyed sly fellow, who stretched out his arms to block her way and then with a leer said:

"Little Cabbage, meet Liu Zihe. He is the son of a very important official."

Zihe marvelled at the beauty before him. She was dressed in her favourite emerald outfit and white apron. So taken was he with her that he bowed with his clasped hands before him.

Xiugu's heart beat with panic, her breast rising and falling quickly.

"You're so beautiful," Liu Zihe exclaimed. "To what family do you belong?"

Qian Baosheng answered: "She's the childbride of the bean-curd vendor Ge Xiaoda. People liken her beauty to a fresh tender little cabbage."

"What a waste," Liu Zihe commented. "A flower stuck on a heap of ox dung!"

Qian answered with a loud guffaw of laughter: "A piece of juicy meat fallen into the jaws of a dog!"

Xiugu quickly made her escape, as Liu stood there like a block of wood. Qian gave him a shove and a knowing wink.

"What's the matter, Master Liu? Has she captured your heart?"

"You must help me, Baosheng," Liu pleaded. "Beauties like that should be in nice surroundings."

"No problem," Qian boasted, "but what about my...?"

"Don't worry," Liu replied.

Peaceful Lane was a long narrow strip between high brick walls. At the corner of the lane stood a two-storey ramshackle building shared by two families. On one floor Little Cabbage lived with her husband-to-be, the bean-curd vendor Ge Xiaoda, his mother and young sister Sangu. In another part of the house lived a cousin's family, Ge Wenqing, his mother and wife.

Xiugu's spirits fell when she saw the families out in the courtyard watching Xiaoda preparing to slaughter a squealing black pig. It made her feel sick and when they sat down that evening to eat some of its meat, she left the table.

A ceremony was being held to commemorate the hundredth day of Xiaoda's father's death. His mother instructed him to go to the local nunnery. Two nuns, one old and one young, were invited to recite Buddhist sutras as they beat a wooden fish to expiate the sins of the dead. Xiaoda knelt amid incense smoke before the tablet with the name of his father written on it.

At home Xiugu sat before the kitchen fire while little seven-year-old Sangu nestled up to her, handing bundles of sticks to keep the fire going. It was a peaceful scene as the flames shone on the beautiful face of Xiugu, but the peace was suddenly broken by the sound of men shouting out in the hall.

The two girls crept near and saw a large man clutching Xiaoda's collar.

"If you have money to pay nuns to pray for the soul of your father, then you can pay back what you owe me," he shouted.

It was Zhou, the proprietor of the local bean-curd

shop who had lent money to pay for Mr. Ge's funeral. He tried to struggle free from the choking hold on his throat, while Mrs. Ge pleaded for leniency. "Give us a few more days," she cried, "and we'll definitely repay the money."

"I've got to have it today," Zhou snarled, and pushed the old woman down.

Little Cabbage and Sangu rushed to help her up. Zhou, on seeing Xiugu, released his hold and stretched out a hairy hand and raised Xiugu's chin. "With such a beautiful childbride, you don't have to worry about repaying," and he gave a dirty laugh. The furore had roused the whole house and the two families surrounded Zhou, begging for a few days' grace. He gave Xiaoda another seven days to repay the debt.

"Duo, duo duo..." came the mournful sound of the wooden fish being beaten by the nuns nearby.

At the entrance of Peaceful Lane, two men — Qian Baosheng and Zhou — were grinning broadly. "I'm afraid, young master Liu can't wait for seven days," Qian said, and laughed.

Xiaoda came into his mother's room. His homespun jacket was slung over his shoulders as he announced he was leaving for work. The shop where he made beancurd was ten kilometres away. "It will be ten days to a fortnight before you return," she said anxiously. "How are we going to pay back the loan?" Xiaoda promised he would ask his employer to lend him the money, but his mother was not reassured. "How will he help? He is evil. He cheated us out of our beancurd shop, when your father died and we had to plead with him to let you work for him. You are like a slave getting up in the small hours to grind the beans."

"I'll try," said Xiaoda, "and let you know."

As he left the house, his mother called after him: "If you can't get the money, don't come home!"

The threats made Mrs. Ge ill again and she was unable to work at the Yang household. Instead, Xiugu took her place and once again she was able to resume her painting and reading lessons given by the kindly Naiwu. Her happiness shone through her natural beauty so much that Naiwu's sister became suspicious.

One day, she said to her brother: "It's been a full year since your wife passed away and the matchmakers have been coming in droves."

"But I'm preparing for the imperial examination in the autumn," Naiwu protested.

"What are your feelings towards Xiugu?" Shuying asked.

"She's clever, intelligent and sweet," he replied.

"What a pity such a pretty girl should be the childbride of the bean-curd maker," she said.

"That's her fate," Naiwu sighed.

"That's just how I feel," his sister replied. "What fate ordains cannot be changed. If she wanted to break the marriage contract to marry someone else, she would have to go through official channels."

"Does she want to?" Naiwu asked.

"I don't know, but what I do know is that women should protect their reputations. Gossip is a fearsome thing."

Naiwu felt as if he had been stabbed.

Shuying continued: "Xiugu is very young. It would be mean to seduce her and ruin her reputation."

Naiwu finally understood her meaning and protested: "Oh no, sister...."

Shuying, mollified, said: "Maybe I'm worrying over nothing, like weeping for people in ancient tragedies."

In a room above the Benevolent Pharmacy, shelves upon shelves were filled with jars of medicinal herbs, powders and pills. Qian Baosheng was lounging on his bed, yawning fitfully, when Liu Zihe walked in. "You've saved my life," Qian called out and produced his opium pipe. Liu held out a paper packet invitingly in his hand. "What about the arrangement you're making for me? It's been five days now."

Qian gave an oily smile. "We still have three days to go, don't worry." He snatched the packet from Liu, flopped down on the bed and started to smoke. Liu waited until he had puffed a few draughts of opium before asking how Qian planned to abduct Xiugu.

"There's the soft way and the hard way," he said. "She'll either come willingly or we'll take her by force."

Liu was dubious.

"My dear Master Liu, your name sounds the same as 'ox', so an ox needs only to open its mouth to eat a cabbage, right?"

"Three more days?" Liu queried.

"You really are in a hurry. Three days isn't too long," Qian replied.

Liu slapped him on the back. "You were really in a sorry state when I came in just now."

It was evening in Naiwu's study. Streaks of smoke curled up from the incense burning before a pure white porcelain statue of the Bodhisattva. Naiwu asked Xiugu: "Is Bodhisattva a man or a woman?" Even a three-year-old knows that, thought Xiugu, and answered: "It's a woman."

"You're wrong. It's neither man nor woman. Or you can say it's both."

"That can't be true," she said.

Naiwu was serious. "I never tell lies," he said. "Bodhisattva was born in India and is actually twin horses who are strong, clever and intelligent. It can make the blind see, mend broken bones, find husbands for widows and save a sinking ship. When Buddhism was introduced into China, its Indian name, meaning twin horses, was translated as Guanshiyin (Goddess of Mercy) because hundreds of years later there grew a legend which describes how a tragic childbride on Putuo Mountain became a nun and after her death, whenever anyone was in trouble, they would chant: 'Benevolent Bodhisattva, deliver us,' and she would appear from the sea with a willow twig in her hand, riding on a turtle's back to Putuo Mountain."

"So she was a childbride too," Xiugu said and her eyes brightened at the similarity.

A coughing sound came from outside the door. Xiugu quickly stood up and lowered her eyes as Shuying entered.

"Have you finished here?" she asked.

"Young mistress," said Xiugu, "the master has been explaining a Buddhist sutra to me so I can explain it to my mother-in-law."

Shuying looked at the statue and commented:

"What a filial daughter-in-law she is." She took her hand and eyed her up and down. "You're becoming more and more beautiful; any man must surely fall in love when he sees you."

Naiwu busied himself with his writing brush and pretended not to hear.

"When you formally become Xiaoda's wife," Shuying said smiling, "I'll come to the wedding."

Embarrassed, Xiugu hurried out of the room.

"What sutras are you teaching that beautiful child?" Shuying asked her brother.

He remained silent.

"I think it would be better if Mrs. Ge came back to work instead. We don't want idle gossip."

Naiwu answered: "A slanted shadow cannot harm an upright man!"

"It's your own good I'm concerned about, brother. Look at her status and yours. Our parents died early. So did your wife. As the only son of the Yangs, we rely on you to achieve high office and bring glory to our ancestors. When you have done that, I shall know I have done my duty."

"What troubles you, little sister, that you go on and on like this?" Naiwu asked.

"It was you who said that the new county magistrate, Liu Xitong, harbours a grudge against you. Wasn't that why you shut yourself away to concentrate on your studies and stopped receiving guests and writing letters of complaints for people?"

"Put your mind at rest," he answered.

"If you say so," Shuying said.

Mrs. Ge came in from Peaceful Lane and passed by her nephew Wenqing's door. His mother beckoned to her.

"Tomorrow is the seventh day," she said, "the deadline for paying back the money. I've heard that Old Zhou is coming to take a hostage. Did you get the money?"

Mrs. Ge turned pale and shook her head.

Wenqing's mother warned: "Xiaoda's employer has refused a loan so make sure he doesn't return and fall into the hands of Old Zhou. But the young master Qian of the Benevolent Pharmacy has a long nose and has come by with an offer of help."

Mrs. Ge cringed. "His money is not good money," she said. "He must be up to something evil. What can we do, with Zhou like a tiger and Qian like a wolf? They are both bloodthirsty." Tears streamed down her face as she cried: "Only Buddha can help us." Wenqing's mother let out a sigh: "Wenqing's teacher's pay only brings in a bushel of rice a month." Her daughter-in-law appeared and removed the jade bracelet from her wrist. "Take this, auntie, and pay the debt."

Mrs. Ge shook her head. "A cup of water can't put out a fire." She went to her room and threw herself down before her husband's memorial tablet and burned incense.

Xiaoda suddenly appeared. Mrs. Ge was taken aback. "Why did you come home?" she demanded. "It's too dangerous. Old man Zhou is bound to get you!"

"I couldn't stay away and let them bully you and Xiugu," with that he looked round for her.

Xiugu was gazing out of the little window of her tiny bedroom, lost in thought. The experiences of the last few days had disturbed her, making her wonder whether she was happy or sad.

Xiaoda came in and clutched her in his arms and tried to kiss her.

The sudden attack frightened her and she struggled and shouted.

"You're mine anyway," he snarled, "why shouldn't I kiss you?"

He released her as he heard his mother call him and he stormed downstairs.

The incident brought a flood of anguish and Xiugu wept as she thought of what the future held for her. Much later, she dried her tears and went down to see Mrs. Ge on her knees before her husband's memorial tablet. "Forgive me, Xiugu," she began, "I see no way out. The debt collector is as fierce as a demon. I've racked my brains to think of a way out and the only thing I can think of..."

Xiugu stood silent and still.

"Go and ask Master Yang Naiwu to come over for a drink of wine at our place tonight."

In the evening Naiwu was seated in the place of honour as Mrs. Ge placed dishes and wine before him. Xiugu sat before him at the candlelit table.

Mrs. Ge picked up a shrimp with her chopsticks and put it on Naiwu's plate. "Have some salted shrimp, Master Yang. I know shrimp and steamed fish are your favourite dishes. Give him some wine, Xiugu."

Xiugu poured out some wine, trying to suppress her

happiness in front of her mother-in-law.

"You have cared for my family," Mrs. Ge said. "When I fell ill you came to treat me and gave me money to buy medicine and allowed Xiugu to work in my place and taught her Buddhist sutras. We can never repay your kindness. Xiugu, pour Master Yang another cup of wine."

"Please don't mention such minor matters," protested Naiwu.

Mrs. Ge instructed Xiugu to pour out more wine, while she went and prepared more dishes.

After several cups of wine Naiwu's face became flushed and he gazed passionately at Xiugu as she went to collect more dishes.

In the kitchen, a desperate Mrs. Ge said: "For the Ge family's sake and for the sake of your husband-to-be, please make the sacrifice. Women are born to suffer. I beg of you, Xiugu…"

Xiugu was frightened as she realized what Mrs. Ge was hinting at and placed her hands to her face in shame. "No, I can't," she said.

Mrs. Ge replied in a cold voice: "Very well, then. Take this dish up and have a drink with him."

Xiugu placed the dish before him, blushing and her heart thumping.

Naiwu mistook her red face for shyness and urged her to drink with him. He raised his cup: "I'm offering you a toast as your teacher, so you must drink with me."

The candles spluttering in the room and the wine made Naiwu feel hot and breathless. He opened the window, looked at the full moon set in the clear sky and softly recited the well-known lines of the Tang Dynasty poet Zhang Jiuling:

> *"A brilliant moon rises above the sea,*
> *You and I, though far apart, gaze at it*
> *The very same moment."*

As he seemed occupied, Xiugu thought to slip out of the room, but the door was locked and on the other side she heard her mother-in-law say in a hoarse whisper:

"Look at me through the crack, my dear daughter."

She was on her knees. "Only you and Master Yang can save our family... If you refuse, Xiugu, I shall remain kneeling...."

Forced into A Liaison

XIUGU turned round and found Naiwu slumped with his arms and head on the table in a drunken stupor.

Like the stormy sea and choppy waters, her heart was in tumult. She loved and respected Naiwu but her reputation would suffer if she let temptation satisfy their desires. He was too drunk to move and her future mother-in-law was still kneeling outside the door, pleading to think of the family's honour.

Wax dripped from the candles like tears; the wooden clapper of the night watchman sounded in the distance. She could not leave him slumped over the table all night, so she dragged him to her bed and lay him down.

The candles burned out and the moon shone through the window on the sleeping man. Xiugu sat like a statue and gazed at the man she loved as her imagination took flight and she saw herself as a bride on her wedding night, the strains of wedding music filling the air. The bridal chamber was lit by two red candles, symbolic of wedded bliss. She sat on the edge of a bed, wearing an embroidered red dress, and her face was covered by a red cloth. A smiling Naiwu was pulling off the scarf from her bowed head, and holding her hand, he was saying to her in a tender voice: "Heaven has granted our wish, Xiugu. You are my wife at last!"

The crowing of a cock startled Xiugu out of her fantasy and Naiwu woke to find he was not in his own bed. Slowly the realization came as he remembered the events of the evening before. He scrambled out of the bed as she brought his shoes.

"I'm so sorry," he said "this is all my fault."

Xiugu, with tears of humiliation, hastened to assure him that the fault was hers. "It is because my family is too poor," she sobbed, "that's why we kept you here."

Naiwu realized that however innocent the night had been, Xiugu's reputation was damaged and he was full of remorse.

"You must really hate me," he said.

"No, no!" protested Xiugu. "How can I hate someone who has been so kind and taught me to read and paint, and explained the Buddhist sutras to me?"

He was moved by her generous spirit and begged her to wait until he had passed the imperial examination to become a *juren**. "Then," he said, "I'll send a matchmaker to ask for your hand in marriage."

Xiugu answered: "I am already betrothed to Ge Xiaoda." He allayed her doubts by promising to pay him off. "He will be able to marry someone else," he said.

The sky in the east was gradually tinged with red.

Sitting at the table, Naiwu composed a poem for Xiugu.

---

*Juren is a title given to a successful candidate in the imperial examinations at provincial level.

> "*A rare beauty as you are*
> *Ought not to have fallen into the dusty world.*
> *Forced into a liaison, we are destined for each other.*
> *Our ties will last like the ever rolling waters.*"

Xiugu, in return, gave him a purse embroidered with two fluttering butterflies.

There was so much more he wanted to say to her.

Meanwhile in a gambling house during that eventful night, the pharmacist, Qian, had been with his gambling friends and there was much yelling and shouting as they flung down their stakes. He was shaking uncontrollably as he slowly fanned out his hand of cards on the table.

"The Earth," he shouted excitedly.

The pot-bellied banker unhurriedly opened his large mouth: "The Heavens. I take all." He raked in all the stakes.

Qian dashed out of the gambling house like a madman.

The sky was now a tint of pale as the door of the Ge household slowly opened. Xiugu peeped out and saw a deserted lane. Naiwu quietly slipped out with his head hidden and hurried away.

How could the two people in love know that the scene had been witnessed by Qian who, after storming out of the gambling house, had entered the lane. An evil smile appeared on his face.

Later, Qian and Liu Zihe began plotting in a room above the Benevolent Pharmacy. Qian told Liu that by making old man Zhou demand repayment of the debt from the Ge family, they had only succeeded in putting the "cabbage into the goat's mouth." Liu was mad with jealousy. "I must have her," he cried, "she has swept me off my feet."

Measuring his words carefully, Qian replied: "When you chase away the 'goat', the 'ox' (which is almost the same sound as his surname 'Liu' in Chinese) will have a chance."

All agog, Liu begged him to reveal his plans.

Qian continued to take his time. "Of course," he drawled.

"Spit it out," Liu demanded.

Qian said meaningfully: "I was unlucky at cards last night."

Liu instantly produced a gold ingot. "A little token," he said. "All I want is Little Cabbage."

The ingot glittered in Qian's greedy eyes. "No problem. No problem at all," he assured Liu.

The night was dark and windy. In the quietness of the late hours, a poster was secretly pasted on the door of the Yang's ancestral temple.

Early the next morning, Naiwu's great-uncle, Yang Qiye, stomped furiously into Naiwu's home. Although in his seventies, he still enjoyed good health and was normally a peaceful man. But today his face was like a stone and he demanded sternly of the old servant: "Summon your master to me."

The servant, Chen Laode, hurried away.

Naiwu entered and addressed him with respect: "Great-uncle."

"You have the nerve to face me?" roared Yang Qiye.

He pulled a sheet of paper from his sleeve and tossed it on the desk. "Take a look," he shouted.

In thick heavy strokes were written the characters: "Goat* Eating Cabbage". Naiwu's face turned scarlet.

Great-uncle's beard quivered in rage. "This disgusting thing was pasted on the door of our ancestral temple. It is an insult to our ancestors and a shame to our clan!"

Naiwu answered quietly: "Xiugu and I are innocent. We have done nothing wrong."

His great-uncle was not satisfied and shouted: "You have brought shame on an old man like me!"

Naiwu's sister came into the room, helped him sit down and gave him tea.

He pointed to the poster: "All the city knows about 'Goat Eating Cabbage'."

Shuying was startled to see the notice written in such bold thick characters, and she started to question her brother, but he shook his head.

"Maybe an enemy is trying to damage your reputation," she said with a sigh. "Xiugu often comes here to study Buddhist sutras and painting. That gives people food for gossip. She must stop coming from now on."

As Great-uncle Qiye nodded, Naiwu spoke up: "Why shouldn't she come to our home? She wants to learn and I'm willing to teach her. Everything is above board. We haven't done anything to be ashamed of."

---

* "Goat", in Chinese, is pronounced exactly the same as "Yang".

Shuying turned pale: "Brother, you shouldn't sacrifice your reputation over the childbride of a bean-curd seller."

Great-uncle Qiye, still very angry, remonstrated: "Compare your family status with her origin. If you have no consideration for the good name of the Yangs, I still mind about my reputation and responsibilities to our ancestors."

Seeing Naiwu was still stubborn, he went into a rage. "Have you forgotten our ancestors and defy the canon and damage our reputation? I will ask the clan leader to open the door of the ancestral temple and give you such a beating, your legs will be broken!"

Shuying hastened to calm down the old man. "You shouldn't upset Great-uncle so, brother," she said.

He raged on: "Since your parents died when you were young, Shuying has brought you up like a mother so that you can become a somebody. We have all pinned our hopes on your passing the imperial examination next year to bring honour to our ancestors and fortune to our family. But you lack self-respect and have caused a scandal. You are unworthy of your dead parents and your sister."

Naiwu bowed his head.

That same morning, as Xiugu's betrothed, Xiaoda, arrived at the end of the lane, he saw a poster on the brick wall. He read: "Goat Eating Cabbage" and as the meaning finally dawned on him, blood rushed to his face and he ran home where he saw his mother and Xiugu working in the kitchen.

He showed his mother the poster. "Goat Eating Cabbage," he shouted in fury. The two women went as pale as ghosts and then Xiugu's face began to turn scarlet. Mrs. Ge was overcome by dizziness and fainted away. She was taken to her bed from which she never rose again.

That same evening, Naiwu came to bid Xiugu farewell. "I'm leaving early tomorrow morning for Suzhou to continue my studies," he told her.

"When will you return?" she asked timidly.

"Six months to a year," he answered.

She felt a sense of foreboding.

"You don't hate me, do you?" he asked.

"No," she answered. "I hate neither heaven nor earth, neither my proposed mother-in-law nor you, only my wretched fate." She broke down in tears.

He wiped her eyes.

"I only regret," said Xiugu, turning away frightened at her boldness, "the false reputation I have of being eaten by a goat," and she blushed furiously.

There was so much he wanted to say again but instead he held her hand and muttered: "My dear Xiugu, please wait for me."

He unwrapped the cloth of the white porcelain statue of Bodhisattva. "In the time while I am away you can recite sutras, write and paint before her. She will bless you...."

She clutched the Bodhisattva against her breast and murmured: "May the benevolent Bodhisattva who delivers us from misery let us be united soon."

The scenery beside the Shaoxi Stream was still beautiful: willow branches swayed in the wind, a pair of butterflies fluttered among the flowers. Xiugu, hiding behind a tree, watched as Naiwu was seen off by his sister. His servant, Chen Laode, accompanied his young master.

He bowed, folding his hands before him. "I want you to do something for me," he said. "Look after Xiugu's mother-in-law."

Shuying was desperate to know more about his relationship with Xiugu, but he boarded the boat before she could say anything.

As the boat moved away, Xiugu stepped from behind the tree and gazed after it, her heart full of foreboding.

Again, she seemed to hear the familiar local song.

"The stream clear and long
Wild flowers on its bank emit a heady fragrance.
A maiden places a flower on her head,
Attracting butterflies to fly in pairs."

Two lines of tears rolled down her face.

She watched until the boat was no longer in sight before returning sadly home.

Mrs. Ge was seriously ill. As Xiugu prepared a herbal tonic for her, Naiwu's sister made an unexpected visit.

The old lady struggled to sit up, protesting at the trouble she was causing but Shuying quickly pacified her and then looked meaningfully at Xiugu, who took the hint and left the room.

"I think Xiaoda and Xiugu are old enough to be man and wife now," she said. "Then you can set your mind at rest that the family line will carry on. Here is a small token from the Yang family for the celebration." She placed ten silver dollars by her bed.

Mrs. Ge understood the real meaning behind her words and blushing she took the money with expressions of gratitude.

That evening, Mrs. Ge called for Xiugu, held her hand and sighed: "Women have come to this world to suffer and bear children," she said. "My days are numbered so I have something I must say to you. The young master of the Yang family is a good man and I know your feelings. But he has a prestigious background; you must not affect his future... Before I breathe my last, you had better move in with Xiaoda," she said.

The request was like a thunderbolt. Xiugu fell to her knees and pleaded: "No, no. Naiwu will come back. He'll definitely come back." Her tears fell like the pearls from a broken necklace and Xiaoda and his sister Sangu came rushing in to find out what all the noise was about.

Xiugu ran down the stairs with her head lowered, tears dancing in her eyes.

Mrs. Ge spoke quietly to her son.

The moon stole quietly into Xiugu's room where she lay sleeping.

Her door was pried open and Xiaoda stole over to her bed. In the moonlight, her full and attractive body made him wild with desire and he threw himself down on her.

Startled, Xiugu awoke to find the usually placid Xiaoda was now rough and panting hard as he tore at her clothes and pressed down on her.

She opened her mouth to scream but a towel was stuffed into her mouth and as the moon became obscured by dark clouds, her struggling gradually died away.

Mrs. Ge's bedroom was now converted into the bridal chamber. It was decorated with a pair of red candles and the character Double Happiness was pasted on the door.

A tearful wooden Xiugu sat with her head lowered. The marriage was consummated and she was now the daughter-in-law of the Ge household. All her dreams and hopes had disappeared like bubbles into thin air. The dull ache within her reminded her of the words her mother-in-law had said. "Women have come to this world to suffer...."

Wearing a long gown and cap, the happy Xiaoda walked over to his bride.

On the top floor of his pharmacy, Qian had prepared a few dishes and was drinking with his crony, Liu Zihe.

Liu was not interested in drinking that night. Instead he grumbled: "You told me that when you drove away the goat, I, the ox, will be able to taste the cabbage. Now that Yang Naiwu has gone, Little Cabbage has become a married woman. A fresh flower on a pile of ox dung, what a waste!"

Qian smiled obsequiously: "Though stuck on ox dung, she is still a fresh flower, an unsurpassed peerless beauty."

Liu's hopes rose. "I'll give you a handsome reward if you get her for me," he said.

Qian replied in measured tones: "Xiugu is not just anybody. She was from a scholarly family. Her father was a teacher before they came here as refugees. She lost her mother and had to sell herself as a childbride when her father died. Yang Naiwu had taught her reading and writing and the Buddhist scriptures. It is not easy to capture the heart of such an intelligent woman."

Liu instantly produced three taels of gold and placed them on the table. "I know you can do anything," he urged.

Qian laughed: "I have already thought of a way to win her for you."

Excited, Liu pleaded: "Tell me quick, how?"

Qian nodded: "Her husband is a bean-curd maker and they're poor. But she does good embroidery and helps to keep the family going with the money she earns. You and I can go as customers and order some embroidery, then you can talk with her."

Liu beamed with joy. "And then?"

"And then? A lot of things can happen..." Qian raised his winecup and tossed the drink back.

Mrs. Ge died a few days later, and the body lay stretched out on the first floor. Xiugu put on mourning dress. They had no money to bury her until Shuying contributed twenty silver dollars. As Xiugu went down on her knees in gratitude, she helped her up and eyed her thin face with compassion: "You should take care of yourself," she said kindly.

A week after the funeral, as Xiugu was embroidering, Qian and Liu entered the premises.

Solemnly, Qian introduced Liu: "This is Young Master Liu. He is getting married."

Xiugu had a feeling they did not mean well, but she could not show her displeasure. It could be a genuine order for work. Liu was too disturbed by her beauty to accept the tea she offered.

"What would the young master like me to embroider?" she asked.

Qian gave Liu a shove as he seemed unable to speak coherently. "What do I want embroidered?" Liu muttered. Then he turned to Qian and whispered: "Tell me quick, what do I want embroidered?"

Covering Liu's confusion, Qian said: "The young master doesn't know much about embroidery. You can make him anything that's suitable for a wedding, like pillow-cases and quilt covers. He'll leave everything to you. Give her an advance, young master."

Liu produced three taels of gold.

Xiugu had never seen so much gold before and protested: "We do not need that much gold to buy materials."

Liu's eagerness to put himself into her good graces was likely to make her suspicious, so when he began to tell her to keep what was left of the gold, Qian hastily intervened by telling her to return what was left and that as his master was very busy they would come another day. He placed the gold on the table and pulled Liu away.

Liu was not at all happy and grumbled: "Why did we leave so quickly?"

"An eager man cannot eat hot bean-curd," was the answer. "Little Cabbage is an intelligent woman. You paid three taels of gold for pillow cases and satin covers, much too much. If her suspicions had been aroused and she had refused the order, you would not be able to visit a second time."

But Liu was not to be appeased.

Qian said persuasively: "I know you wish to have her as soon as possible. I have something up my sleeve which will guarantee that wish in three days, with no resistance from her at all. She will be yours to do as you want."

Liu was ecstatic. "Tell me quickly," he said.

He answered: "I have some very precious medicine. But it's very expensive."

"How about a hundred silver dollars?" asked Liu.

Qian slapped his thigh: "It's a deal," he said.

Three days later, they visited Xiugu again. Liu was dressed in his best and they greeted her cordially while she made them tea. Qian insisted she join them in a cup and Liu asked to see her work. Xiugu went upstairs to get the embroidery and while she was out of the room, Qian quickly produced a small package and poured the contents into her cup.

She returned with pillow-cases embroidered with Mandarin ducks and drakes, symbolizing a loving couple. Liu was full of praise.

Qian gave her the cup. "You have worked very hard," he said. "Please drink your tea."

With one man praising her, the other offering her tea so politely, she accepted the tea without the slightest suspicion. They smiled as she drank and began to make signs of leaving, when Liu suddenly tripped and fell. He cried out with pain and seemed unable to move. Qian looked serious. "He may have broken his leg," he said. "Ask your sister-in-law to come with me to the pharmacy for medicine. Then I'll find a bone-setter."

Shortly after Qian and Sangu left, Xiugu began to feel dizzy and objects in the room seem to be floating. But the strangest sensation of all was Liu standing up. He closed the door and turned back towards her.

Xiugu felt her legs turn to jelly and was unable to

move. She saw pictures of the Ghost Festival — big-headed ones, small-headed ones, with blue faces and fangs — swooping over her with sinister laughter.... She screamed in fear and collapsed.

Liu caught her and held her in his arms....

Slaughter A Goat and Frame It

XIUGU did not know how long she had remained unconscious, but as she came to she felt limp, like a piece of chewed cotton. She turned her head and made out the figure of a man lying beside her. It was Liu Zihe! She was paralysed with fear and tried to sit up, but did not have the strength.

Liu moved his grinning face towards her and she quickly pulled some clothes over her naked breasts. When Liu said in a sugary voice: "Sister." She gave him a sharp slap across the face and then burst into tears.

"Heaven will not forgive you," she cried.

He took a jade ring off his finger and offered it to her, but she threw it to the floor. He placed several ingots of gold on the table but she brushed those off as well.

There was a loud knocking at the door. He leapt out of bed and grabbed the gold and ring. It was Sangu who opened the door and demanded why it had been closed.

Liu stammered his excuses and pretended to limp away.

When she shouted after him: "What about this medicine?" he did not reply but hurried his steps, no longer limping.

She hurried upstairs to find a tear-stained Xiugu with

her clothes in disarray who clutched her in a tight embrace and wailed.

The weather changed suddenly and a wind blew down from the mountains.

In the mulberry garden at the back of their house, a sad-faced Xiugu stared at a hollow section of bamboo in a pool of muddy water. As dirty water gurgled into the bamboo, Xiugu quickly turned her face away.

Wenqing's wife and her mother-in-law were dyeing cloth outside the back door. When some of the dye splashed out, Wenqing's wife cried: "Oh my, my sleeve is stained!" Her mother-in-law replied: "It will never wash clean again."

Xiugu's face twitched and she hung her head down in shame.

She walked deeper into the mulberry orchard where she came to a stone well. She saw her reflection in the cold water and remembered again her mother-in-law's words as she lay dying: "Women have come to this world to suffer."

Xiugu felt her chest tighten. She was nineteen years old and hadn't had much out of life, yet today she was going to leave this world, hoping that the clear water would wash away all her shame....

The crows cawed noisily overhead as they flew back to their nest. Now was the time! She prepared to jump in but her legs were suddenly grabbed from behind by Sangu, who cried out: "Mother has already left us ... I'll not tell anyone, sister-in-law. I promise!"

They clutched each other and cried.

The wind tore through the mulberry branches, shaking them vigorously. Heavy drops of rain poured down from the sky in a never-ending stream onto a miserable little world.

Summer was passing, giving way to autumn. Yang Naiwu's Great-uncle had died and he returned for the funeral. When he heard Xiugu was married he fell into a deep melancholia and left home again as soon as it was possible to do so.

He came to the banks of the Shaoxi Stream where he and Xiugu had first met....

In the distance the masculine and the feminine pagodas stood, unchanged by time, but for Naiwu, life had taken a dramatic turn for the worse.

Xiugu was walking slowly up the steps from the stream with a basket of freshly washed vegetables. She had cut off her glossy black plait and now wore her hair in a bun like all married women did. She was still wearing her favourite green outfit. She halted suddenly, her heart beat rapidly and her face turned red when she saw the familiar figure of Naiwu — still handsome, still dignified as ever.

It was an unexpected encounter for Naiwu too. He saw she was now more beautiful as a woman than she had been as a girl.

Xiugu spoke first: "Are you going away already?" she asked.

Naiwu replied bitterly: "Although Yuhang County is large, there is no place for me."

"It was all my fault," she said sadly.

"It is fate that has ordained that I can't be with you... Heaven and earth are not to blame, nor you or my family."

He was repeating almost the same words she had

said the night she had pledged to wait for him. But where could she begin? Instead she said: "Bodhisattva has not blessed or protected me...."

Naiwu's manservant, Chen Laode, interrupted them: "Mrs. Ge, the young master has to leave for Hangzhou to prepare for the imperial examination."

Xiugu forced a smile. "I wish the young master every success and hope he becomes a..." Naiwu finished her sentence "... a *juren*. Then," she smiled, "I can address you as Your Honour."

She felt the distance between Naiwu and herself growing ever wider.

He seemed insensitive to the tumult within her, as he thanked her. Suddenly they heard a shepherd boy call out in a shrill voice: "Look, a goat eating the cabbage."

A white goat, attracted by the vegetables in Xiugu's basket, was eating a cabbage.

As if stung by a bee, the two parted quickly and went their ways.

The chilly light of the waning moon shone on the white porcelain Bodhisattva which Naiwu had given Xiugu. She gazed at it, puzzled why the benevolent goddess had made her an exception and not blessed or protected her.

She put down her sewing and opened her comb and hairpin box and removed from the bottom a sheet of paper which she had secreted from prying eyes. It was a poem he had written for her. She turned up the oil-lamp and read it again.

"*A rare beauty as you are*
Ought not have fallen into a dusty world.

*Forced into a liaison, we are destined for each other.
Our ties will last like the ever rolling water."*

Yang Naiwu passed the imperial examination at provincial level later that year and was given the title of *juren*.

His residence was a scene of bustle and excitement. The gate was wide open and musical instruments played merry tunes. The neighbours came to watch the happy event. A government messenger in red felt hat and black costume, holding high a red scroll, arrived at the Yang household to announce the results. At the top of his voice he shouted: "His Excellency Yang Naiwu of your honourable household has come one hundred and fourth in the imperial examination and is now a *juren*."

Fireworks were let off and gongs and drums were beaten. Amid loud applause and congratulations, Yang Naiwu, his face glowing with happiness, thanked the neighbours and relatives, with his hands held high in front of him.

When the celebrations were over he burned incense and bowed before the memorial tablets of his ancestors. Wiping away her tears of happiness, his sister, Shuying, said to him: "You have brought glory to our family. Our dead parents would be pleased with your success. Tonight we must give a party for our neighbours, relatives and friends."

He called on every household in the area and at last reached the home of Xiugu. Her husband, Xiaoda, was just entering the lane when he saw his beautiful wife at the gate with Naiwu, who was in high spirits. He hid himself behind a pillar and heard them talking.

"I called you Your Honour a few months before

your examination," she said.

He replied: "I owe my success to your good wishes. Tonight I shall toast you three times."

Xiugu was hesitant: "Tonight ... my husband isn't home...."

Naiwu laughed: "Then the invitation is extended. We can still see each other."

As Xiaoda eavesdropped he at last understood the meaning of the phrase: "Goat eating cabbage. Goat eating cabbage."

Naiwu's happy laughter echoed in his ears: "The invitation is extended. We can still see each other."

He walked with unsteady steps to the front door of his home, as the latch slid to. The thought of being shut out of his own home maddened him and he raised his fists to hammer at the door, but then thought better of it, turned away and shambled out of the lane full of anger and revenge.

As he walked out of the lane into the main street, his arm was suddenly caught. It was the local grocer who invited him for a drink but in reality wanted him to slaughter his goat.

Xiaoda was a well-known butcher, working fast and efficiently — with just one stab of the knife, it was done. He downed three cups of wine and grabbed a knife.

In the courtyard, a trussed-up goat was bleating pitifully.

He grabbed the goat's head in his left arm and with a swift plunge of the knife, it was done. As he pulled out the knife, a thick spurt of blood shot out. He wiped it clean on the goat's fur and stared intently at the gleaming knife.

The main hall at the Yang's household was lit up and a group of musicians was playing lively music. It was filled with guests who had come to offer their congratulations. Yang Naiwu raised his winecup: "I owe this happy occasion to all my elders and neighbours for the love and concern you have all shown me. Let me offer a toast to you all." The guests all raised their cups.

At another table, Shuying sat with Wenqing's mother and his wife. Wenqing's mother whispered to Shuying: "I hear that the new *juren* is taking a wife in a few days?" Shuying nodded happily. Wenqing's mother, congratulating, said: "Then it is another happy occasion — really true Double Happiness."

Downing several more cups of wine at the grocer's home had made Xiaoda less hurt by what he had seen earlier and he started off home slightly drunk. The night was black and the moon was obscured by a passing cloud, so that the lane was in darkness except for a light which shone from his wife's window — and he saw the silhouettes of a man and a woman. He listened and could hear a man's voice. Overcome by rage at apparently finding his suspicions confirmed, his eyes became murderous.

Inside the room was Xiugu's seducer, Liu Zihe, who was pestering her again. Xiugu angrily told him to leave, warning him that her aunt was only next-door. Liu grinned. "They are all at the celebrations at Yang Naiwu's house," he said. Xiugu tried another tack: "My husband will be home any minute." Liu was undeterred. "Your husband will not be home for a fortnight," he said confidently.

Xiaoda stole round to the back-door, took a twig

from a willow tree and jammed it into the latch from the outside.

Liu had already taken off his long gown and was sitting on the edge of Xiugu's bed. He put his gold watch under the pillow, while his lecherous eyes swept her figure as though he would crush Xiugu in his arms. Xiugu pleaded with him to leave her alone, but her entreaties only inflamed him more. As he drew closer to her, Xiugu cried out furiously: "Aren't you worried...?"

He laughed derisively: "Worried about what? My father will be county magistrate for another three years." He grabbed her and pushed her roughly onto the bed. She struggled as he tore at her clothes, but then a loud knocking was heard downstairs. Liu went pale.

"Open the door quickly," Xiaoda called. Grabbing his clothes, Liu made for the back-door. He broke out into a cold sweat as he found it would not open, and darted into Sangu's room. Shaking, Xiugu, came downstairs, removed the wooden bolt on the front-door and slid the wooden latch to one side. Xiaoda pushed the door wide and glared at his wife as he walked in. Although her heart was thumping, she forced a smile. He closed the door and took the long wooden bolt as he searched the room.

"What ... what are you looking for?" asked Xiugu as the colour drained from her face. He did not answer but shoved her aside, ordering her to lead with the lamp and light the way upstairs. She moved reluctantly as he followed her. At the door of their bedroom, as she made way for him, she shook with fear. His eyes fell on the double bed, swathed in the folds of a white mosquito net. He thought he saw something moving. "Bring the lamp over," he ordered loudly. Xiugu did not move. "It's midnight. Don't disturb the neighbours. Tomorrow..." pleaded Xiugu. Ignoring her, Xiaoda lifted the mosquito net, but only found that the bed was uncrumpled. He looked under the bed but saw no-one.

Liu Zihe started to sneak out of Sangu's room and grope his way downstairs. But the worn steps creaked under his weight and hearing this, Xiaoda dashed out of Xiugu's room. The fleeing Liu missed a step and tumbled. Despite the pain, he fled through the front door and took to his heels. Xiaoda picked up a knife from the kitchen and gave chase. Just twenty paces separated the two men. The one in front, in a long gown, his pigtail flying behind him, was being chased by a furious husband — who caught up with him and lunged forward with his knife. Liu cried out in fear, but fortunately for him, Xiaoda stumbled and fell and by the time he got up, Liu was out of sight.

Xiaoda rushed to the east where a pork dumpling stall stood beneath a dim street lamp. He asked if the owner had seen a man running for life. The owner shook his head, so Xiaoda ran to the west. Approaching the Shaoxi bridge, Xiaoda saw several well-dressed young scholars coming in his direction from the celebrations at Yang Naiwu's house. They each held a lantern as they strolled along. One young scholar was saying: "What stroke of luck for him, Yang Naiwu is now a *juren*."

"He'll be able to wear an official red gown instead of ordinary blue," commented another, "his future is now secure."

Liu had already joined the group. He strutted towards Xiaoda and asked him: "Are you chasing after a robber?" "I'm slaughtering a goat," Xiaoda answered in a huff. Liu grinned and sauntered away with the group.

Xiaoda continued his search but to no avail. Still burning with anger and sweating hard he undid the buttons of his tunic to cool himself in the night breeze as he stomped off home.

When he entered the bedroom, Wenqing's mother and wife, Sixth Uncle and Sangu were sitting with Xiugu. He grabbed her and raised his knife but was stopped by the others who tried to wrest the weapon out of his hand. Sangu hid behind Wenqing's wife and cried with fear. After a violent struggle, Xiaoda was disarmed. "Why do you want to kill your wife?" Sixth Uncle asked.

"She's a whore!" Xiaoda replied. Wenqing's mother commented: "You drink yourself silly and then you bully your wife?" Xiaoda spoke through clenched teeth: "Ask her who ran away from her bedroom just now." Sixth Uncle demanded: "Who was it?" Xiaoda roared: "Yang Naiwu."

Wenqing's mother hit him on the shoulder. "Nonsense. Mr. Yang was busy celebrating today. How could he have come here? You must have imagined it."

No-one seemed to believe him and he stamped his foot in rage, unable to give any details. Glaring at his wife he stuttered: "You ... you...." Although tears were streaming down her face, Xiugu still managed to pluck up courage to ask him: "You claim my lover was Mr. Yang. What proof do you have?" "'You dare question me? You whore!" he yelled and lunged towards her.

She threw herself down on her knees before the statue of Bodhisattva. Xiaoda dashed forward and grabbed the porcelain statue. "I know this was a gift from your lover," he snarled. He raised it high and smashed it to the ground where it broke into pieces.

With all her hopes dashed, Xiugu snatched up a pair of scissors to cut off her long hair. "Let me become a nun," she wailed, but Wenqing's mother took the scissors away from her and Sixth Uncle pushed Xiaoda out of the room.

With his hysterical wife threatening to become a nun, a defeated Xiaoda stomped downstairs.

The storm abated and only a sob could be heard now and then in the quiet night from Xiugu's bedroom. What had fate in store for this helpless woman who had been so cruelly seduced?

Murder the Husband to Get the Wife

THE two cronies, Liu Zihe and Qian Baosheng, were in close confabulation in the room above the pharmacy.

"It was narrow escape last night," said Liu. "That stupid husband nearly got me with his knife."

Qian teased: "It would have been a romantic death to be killed for love."

"I'd be dead now, if I hadn't have been so clever," Liu replied.

"You're the son of the county magistrate. He wouldn't dare!" said Qian.

"I was scared, I was cold and it was midnight. My health will suffer if things go on like this," Liu moaned.

"Then repent and take a turn for the better," said Qian.

"What, and give up such a beauty as Little Cabbage? I would rather die!"

"Then you and Ge Xiaoda cannot co-exist. If you want to have her for ever, he will have to die."

Liu nodded his head.

Qian assumed an affected manner and said: "I think you had better forget about Little Cabbage and let them enjoy married life."

Liu gritted his teeth and uttered: "I must get rid of the husband."

Qian said with a smile: "He is very healthy and

strong. There's no likelihood of him dying suddenly, unless...."

Liu said in a wheedling tone: "You could do such a good job, no-one would ever know."

Qian jumped up and protested: "No, no, no, my dear young sir. Murder is a capital crime."

Liu said: "With official posts and money, all cases can be solved. My father is, after all, the magistrate of this county. What do you have to fear?" He took out three ingots of gold from his pocket. "These three taels of gold are worth about a hundred silver dollars."

Qian stared greedily at the shining gold.

"I'll make it worth your while," Liu said.

Qian thought for a moment and then opened a cupboard and took out a blue-patterned white porcelain jar. A red label bore the word: "Arsenic".

They smiled at each other knowingly.

Another bout of illness brought Xiaoda home on sick leave. Xiugu went to help him into the house, but he pushed her away and she fell onto a chair. His young sister felt his forehead. "You're feverish," she exclaimed.

Xiugu was worried and asked Wenqing's mother for advice, who offered to fetch Yang Naiwu. "Only he treats people free of charge and gives medicine," she said.

Xiaoda was convinced that if Naiwu treated him he would die but he was over-ruled by his relatives; unable to resist any more, he gave in.

Naiwu still wore his civilian clothes and did not flaunt his position as a successful imperial scholar. He sat on the edge of the bed and felt Xiaoda's pulse. After examining him, he said that Xiaoda's illness was due to anger going to the liver and he had then caught a chill.

Naiwu spoke quietly to Wenqing's mother: "A red line runs through his tongue. It's very dangerous."

A tearful Xiugu stood nearby.

Naiwu wrote out a prescription. "It will help ease the inflammation of the liver," he said. "Take it to the pharmacy and put it on my account."

When Naiwu paid a second visit he was able to reassure Xiugu that her husband was much better.

"We owe all this to your good treatment," Xiugu said gratefully.

As he was leaving for Hangzhou that day, he gave her another prescription, also to be put on his account at the pharmacy. Xiugu sent her young sister-in-law to collect the medicine from the Benevolent Pharmacy, where Qian, with an air of great concern, asked after her brother. He took the prescription, telling his assistant much to that young man's surprise that he would fill it himself.

Qian weighed the different kinds of herbs and poured them out onto a small piece of paper to be wrapped up. While Sangu looked curiously at the small piles of medicinal herbs on the counter, and at the rows of eye-catching white porcelain jars with blue patterns, Qian nipped upstairs and unlocked a cupboard. He took out some arsenic from a jar and when he returned surreptitiously mixed the powder with the other herbs.

Sangu handed over the package to Xiugu who poured one dose into an earthernware pot, boiled it for an hour and poured the liquid into a bowl for Xiaoda to drink.

He had recovered well from his illness and was able to walk about. As he took the bowl, he grasped her hand and said: "It was my misfortune that I should marry a wife as beautiful as you. Tell me the truth — even if I were to die now, I would be a contented ghost — who was it that night?"

Xiugu's face went from red to pale and pale to red again.

He pulled out the gold watch from under the pillow. "Whose is this?"

She lowered her head but he continued: "I can tell from the last few days that you really wish me to get well. In future, you mustn't go out unless it is really important and I'll give up drinking and not waste a single penny, but give my money to you, and we'll lead a peaceful life. What do you say?"

She nodded. "Take the medicine now."

As he drank the liquid, he said: "I know who it was even if you do not tell."

He pulled a face at the bitter taste and sighed as he drained it down.

As she sat by his bedside patching his jacket, he was suddenly gripped by an excruciating pain. His face went white, his eyes became bloodshot and beads of cold sweat stood out on his forehead. He began to roll about in agony. As his eyes fell upon the concerned face of his wife, he imagined he saw the face of a demon and cried out: "I had forgiven you, yet you…"

As she went to help him, he pushed her away with his last remaining strength. Blood dripped from the corners of his mouth. He wiped it with his hand, realizing that he was dying. As his wife knelt beside him, he stared at the gold watch in his hand and with his last breath uttered the name: "Yang." Blood gushed from his mouth as he dropped back onto the bed, lifeless.

When Xiaoda's cousin, Wenqing, heard the news of his death, he wanted to know the exact nature of his death. His mother told him that he had had a sudden attack at midnight and had died before daybreak.

"Didn't you go over to see him when he got worse?" Wenqing asked. His wife answered: "Sister-in-law Xiugu wanted to come and seek mother's help but Xiaoda didn't want it."

Wenqing was not satisfied and asked if Sangu had been awake then, only to be told that she had slept through the final hours of Xiaoda's life.

"Xiugu was the only person around. That seems very odd," he said.

When he came out of his room he saw funeral couplets written on white paper pasted on the door of his cousin's home. Paper money and sprigs of mugwort hung at the door frame. Two mourning sticks of incense used by relatives of the deceased stood beside the door, ashes of burned paper money and paper ingots lay on the ground.

A blood-red setting sun disappeared behind the mountains leaving a dim and doleful air over everything. Wenqing walked round to the mulberry orchard at the back of the house where the sound of crows cawing grated on his ears. Ahead in a recess of the orchard two figures were whispering, their faces hidden by the swaying mulberry leaves. He heard a man's voice say: "Why do you accuse me of murdering your husband?" and the voice of Xiugu answer: "He died with blood oozing out of his eyes, nose, ears and mouth."

"What's that got to do with me?" Liu Zihe demanded.

She looked at his arrogant and cunning face: "Sangu told me that Qian Baosheng made out the prescription himself."

Liu confessed that he had to go to such extremes in order to possess her for ever.

She threatened to report him but he laughed out loud: "Go ahead. Go and lodge a complaint against me in my father's *yamen**."

Angry though she was, Xiugu realized that she did not stand a chance against such odds and her weak response was to predict that he would not come to a good end. Suddenly Liu heard someone coming and hurried away.

When Wenqing came into the orchard, he only caught a glimpse of a man and a woman as they disappeared. He recognized Xiugu but not Liu.

He searched the orchard in vain and eventually sat by an old well to ponder over the death of his cousin.

In the morning he took Sangu aside and questioned her: "While your brother was away at the bean-curd store, did any man come to see your sister-in-law?" She shook her head and ran off. He was very disturbed at not getting any satisfactory answers to his questions, and the cawing of the crows annoyed him as he leaned against a big tree. Not far away, a

---

*Government office in feudal China.

dog was scratching the ground beneath a mulberry tree. At first, he ignored it but when the dog dug out a jacket stained with blood, he became alert. Another dog came and wrestled with the first dog over the jacket. He chased them off and picked it up.

When he returned home he put the jacket on the table and when his mother saw it she broke down and cried: "I never thought she would do anything so blatantly against public morals with so cruel a deed. I gave him the lining for that jacket," she said tearfully. "I'm going to have it out with her." But Wenqing stopped her.

"As the saying goes: don't lodge a case without proof. With proof in hands, stay away from confrontation. Otherwise the guilty couple will run away. We must write a formal complaint to the *yamen*.

The right person to write the complaint would be Yang Naiwu, thought Wenqing. He went to his home where he found it was bustling with activities. It was the eve of Naiwu's wedding day. A huge character standing for Double Happiness in glittering gold was pasted in the centre of the wall of the main hall and flanked by long red silk on either side printed with good wishes. A glass awning was over the front courtyard under which was a table. Palace lanterns hung in the hall and in the corridor outside the hall charcoal flames leapt up beneath a large copper kettle.

Chen Laode, the old servant, hurried over and when he discovered what Wenqing wanted, he said: "My master has already antagonized the magistrate of Yuhang County and so he decided not to write any more complaints on behalf of anyone but to shut himself away and study. That was how he was able to pass the imperial examination and achieved his present high position." He pointed to the decorations and went on: "Besides, my master is getting married tomorrow. You had better go to someone else." Wenqing muttered: "So Mr. Yang will not redress the wrong done to my cousin."

Firecrackers went off and people cried: "The dowry has been brought over." Young men in pairs carried cases and boxes of household goods. It was a splendid sight winning approval from the on-lookers.

Wenqing elbowed out of the bustling crowd, and made his way to the Yuhang *yamen*.

Two magnificent stone lions crouched outside the closed gate of the *yamen* which made Wenqing feel insignificant as he stepped timidly in at the side-door.

In a pavilion beside a lotus pond, County Magistrate Liu Xitong, the father of Zihe, lay on a couch while his concubine, reclining opposite, prepared his opium pipe. His servant walked in, bowed and reported that a school teacher was outside and wanted to lodge a complaint.

Displeased with the interruption, he grumbled: "Can't you see I'm busy?"

As the servant turned to go, the concubine stopped him. She reminded Liu of his duties as a magistrate: "It is the people you oversee who supply us with our food and clothing," she reminded him.

"Is it about dividing property?" the magistrate asked.

The servant answered: "A man claims that his cousin was murdered by his wife."

The startled Liu sat up abruptly, afraid that if he made a wrong move in a murder case it could affect his official position.

The concubine was intrigued: "I'll listen in," she thought to herself and hid behind a screen.

Ge Wenqing knelt before the magistrate. "My cousin's wife named Xiugu has murdered her husband. I want your excellency to investigate and avenge his death."

Liu glanced at the written complaint and threw it back. "I can't accept it," he said.

"Please have mercy," Wenqing pleaded.

"Who is the seducer of your cousin's wife?" Liu asked.

"I don't know," answered Wenqing. "If Your Excellency will look into the case, that despicable woman will definitely own up if she is tortured."

"To catch a thief, you find the goods; to expose adultery you catch the pair. Without proof, you are committing the crime of perjury," said the magistrate.

"I have a blood-stained jacket as proof," said Wenqing.

"Was the jacket on the body of your cousin?"

"No."

"Was it found in his bedroom?"

"No."

"Did you find it in the street?"

"Yes."

"Something picked up is no evidence, you scoundrel," Liu Xitong scolded. "Take him away, flog him forty times and throw him out."

"Oh my lord," blubbered Wenqing, "my mother recognized the blue lining of the jacket. I beg you to have the coffin opened and the body examined."

The magistrate warned him that he could be beheaded if nothing suspicious was found.

Wenqing was prepared to take the consequences and the magistrate gave orders for the corpse to be exhumed.

The magistrate's concubine helped him on with his official robes, flattering him as she did so: "You are like the upright Magistrate Bao in history; I'm sure you'll rise to greater heights."

Liu Xitong puffed up with conceit.

A tent of blue cloth was erected before the temple. Inside sat the magistrate before a desk. Some distance away the body of Xiaoda was being examined.

The coroner's report stated that he had died of arsenic poisoning.

The magistrate kept his distance and went through the motions of checking and then turning to Wenqing he said: "It seems you are right. You have not been a scholar for nothing. You have dared to come to court to have justice done for your cousin. I will certainly find out the murder and avenge your cousin's death."

Wenqing knelt and struck his head on the ground again and again. "You are a fine magistrate, meting out justice for the people. I hope your family will be officials for many generations."

Qian Baosheng, who had been among the spectators, shook with fright, as Liu Xitong ordered the court runners to arrest the adulteress Xiugu at once.

The reception room of the *yamen* was brightly lit. Awe-inspiring court runners stood at either side of the hall.

Xiugu in chains knelt in front of Liu Xitong who ordered her to raise her head. He expected a murderess to be an ugly shrew but his heart missed a beat when he saw how beautiful she was. He pulled himself together and began questioning her.

"Why did you poison him, if as you say there was love and respect between you?"

"I didn't poison him," Xiugu protested.

He banged his gavel: "You are a brazen hussy. I have had the coffin opened and discovered your husband was poisoned by arsenic. Who was your lover?"

The court runners shouted in response to intimidate her further.

Qian Baosheng was as anxious as a cat on hot bricks, fearing that Xiugu might confess who the real culprits were. He waited impatiently for Liu Zihe's return to Yuhang from Hangzhou by boat.

"Disaster has befallen us," he shouted as he dragged Liu off to the *yamen*.

When they arrived at the hall, they peeped through the door. They heard Zihe's father ask Xiugu where she had obtained the arsenic.

"Who is the adulterer?" the magistrate demanded.

Colour drained from his son's face as he heard his father threaten Xiugu with torture if she did not own up.

Qian pulled at Zihe's sleeve. "Ask your father to adjourn."

Liu was too frightened to move when he suddenly slapped his thigh, muttering: "That's it!" and raced towards the inner quarters of the *yamen*.

Place One Man's Blame on Another

INCENSE smoke rose before a statue of Bodhisattva in a small hall in the inner quarters of the *yamen*. The kneeling figure of Mrs. Liu, the magistrate's wife, was praying before the statue, as a breathless Liu Zihe dashed in and threw himself on his knees before his mother. Startled, she inquired: "Has someone bullied you, my child? Get up quickly."

He wouldn't rise but put on a tearful and pitiful face. "I'm an undutiful son and will not be able to look after you when you are old," he cried. "I'm kneeling to you for the last time!"

In answer to her worried queries, he confessed everything.

Her husband was still in the process of interrogating Xiugu. His ruthless court runners had produced an instrument of torture — a finger-crusher made of bamboo — and Xiugu's fingers were placed in it.

"Own up, you whore!" he demanded.

She remembered Zihe's laughter as he boasted about his father's term of office lasting another three years. "Go ahead," he had threatened, "Lodge a complaint..." How could she tell the magistrate the truth?

Liu Xitong angrily snapped the order: "Tighten the instrument!"

She fainted with the pain and he was about to order that cold water be thrown over her when his servant brought a teacup with a lid. When he lifted the lid he saw a note with the message: "The mistress wants you to adjourn."

He pulled a face and whispered to his servant: "Can't you see that I'm interrogating a murder suspect?"

The servant replied: "The mistress says it's a matter of life and death. Please come to the inner quarters."

He adjourned the interrogation.

As soon as Liu Xitong stepped into the Buddhist hall, he demanded the reason for her urgent message. His wife told him that it was their own son who was the adulterer. The apple of her eye. His son was standing before him with head bowed and his hands beside him — and the magistrate knew his wife was telling the truth. In a rage, he struck his son across the face. "You animal!" he spat out. "How come that the Liu family should have such an evil creature as you!" His beard quivered and he raised his hand to strike again.

His wife moved to protect her son: "Do you want to kill him, you old devil?"

Liu Xitong beat his chest in remorse as tears rolled down his face. "I haven't brought him up properly. I have brought dishonour to my ancestors!"

Mrs. Liu hastened to calm him: "Our ancestors will bless my son so that he will get over this disaster unharmed." She began counting her beads. Her husband stamped his foot: "Why didn't you tell me everything earlier, so that when Ge Wenqing first filed the complaint, I could have turned it down. I could have even ordered the coroner to make out his report as a natural death. But now the whole county suspects that it is Little Cabbage who has murdered her husband and the details have been sent up to the higher level *yamen*. What can I do now when things have gone this far?"

His wife was annoyed: "Then you tie up your own son and take him to the provincial *yamen*. Everyone will know that the magistrate of Yuhang is so upright that he would even have his own son killed to uphold justice. Go ahead and exchange your son for higher office. The family line of the Lius will be cut off and you'll have no descendants." Then she pointed at her son and said: "Go ahead and tie him up!"

Liu Xitong subsided like a punctured balloon. He rubbed his hands and shuffled his feet, unable to decide.

"Even if I do not care for my future, it would be..." he said as though to himself.

Mrs. Liu replied: "I don't care about your future. I want my son. You have been paying a salary to your secretary. Why don't you seek his help at a time like this?"

Secretary Zhao was experienced in criminal law, and was one of the most prestigious secretaries in the *yamen*. He was called upon to deal with the most serious cases in the county. He wondered what merited such an urgent summons at so late an hour. Liu Xitong, forgetting the dignity befitting a magistrate, went straight into the details of the interrogation of Little Cabbage.

"I have discovered who the adulterer is," he said eagerly.

"How efficient and wise you are," Secretary Zhao replied.

"The adulterer is m... is my son. If I had two sons I would have this one tied up and taken to prison. But with the case going this far I am at a loss what to do. I want you to think of a way out for me."

Zhao paced the floor. "Your son is the adulterer. Is he the murderer as well or has he an accomplice? The law of the Qing Government stipulates that an adulterer, if not a murderer, is flogged a hundred times and exiled three thousand *li* away. If the adulterer is a murderer as well, he is beheaded and the woman cut thirty-six times before she dies."

Liu Zihe and his mother, who were hiding behind the curtains, shuddered and came out into the hall. Mrs. Liu, ignoring formalities, went straight to the point. "If you can turn things round and save my son, I will give you a big reward, Secretary Zhao."

Zhao stroked his whiskers and thought for a while. "A stunning beauty like Little Cabbage must be flighty. Does she have other lovers besides you?"

Liu Zihe thought for a moment and said: "No". He was asked to think again. Liu then remembered that when she was a childbride, people had said something about "Goat eating cabbage," and before she was married, she and Yang Naiwu had been in love.

Liu Xitong said: "You mean the new *juren*?" His son nodded. Liu Xitong said to his secretary: "Do you know, I harbour a grudge against Yang Naiwu," and went on to relate what had happened many years ago.

At that time, the magistrate was a grain collecting official in a distant town. There was an unfair practice by which farmers were cheated out of their grain. They had to pour it into a container until the grain was heaped up high. Then the official would give the container three kicks. What spilled out from the heap onto the mat went to the depot instead of the government.

Once, an old farmer began to sweep up what was on the mat and a young official gave him a hard kick and shouted at him. The old farmer tried to reason with the official but only received another kick and was told: "If you sweep that up, what are we going to eat?"

He was badly hurt and blood dripped from his mouth, but the farmer dared not protest.

Yang Naiwu was passing by and helped the old farmer up and asked: "Why mustn't he sweep up the grain?"

Since Naiwu wore a scholar's gown, he could not be ignored and so the young official replied reluctantly: "When handling silver, one makes allowances for wastage in firing. There is wastage in collecting grain too. Don't you know the regulations?"

Naiwu was not intimidated: "The Qing Government has stipulated that the grain container must not be kicked. The provincial government has announced what overflows belongs to the deliverer of the grain."

At this point, Liu Xitong came over to find out what all the trouble was about, but as he was an unprepossessing kind of man, Naiwu did not pay much attention to him and turning to the farmers said in a loud voice: "The provincial *yamen* has stipulated clearly that all that overflows from the container belongs to the deliverers of the grain."

Farmers rushed up to sweep up the spilled grain,

pushing the protesting Liu Xitong aside. Flopping down on the ground he hissed: "Yang Naiwu, I'm not finished with you yet."

That night an indignant Naiwu went in the dark of night to paste a couplet on the vermillion gate of the county *yamen*:

> "*The Qing Government's regulations are not followed*
> *Nor is the announcement of the provincial government.*"

When the provincial government learned about the incident, Liu was removed from office. A few years later, using his wife's money, he bought the post of a magistrate in Yuhang County. Although there were two wealthier counties in the province, he wanted revenge, no matter how long it took. Now with this present case, Yang Naiwu had at last fallen into his clutches. How small the world was!

Blue veins throbbed on Liu Xitong's temples as he recounted his grudge against Yang Naiwu to his secretary. "If you can pin the murder my son committed onto Yang Naiwu, I'll give you a thousand silver dollars."

Zhao was flabbergasted. Never before had he earned so much money.

Mrs. Liu cut in: "If you can save my son's life, I'll give you a thousand dollars, too."

Trying hard to conceal his joy over this unexpected fortune, Zhao folded his hands before him again: "One thousand dollars from each of you is a great deal of money. But this is a complicated case. Yang

Naiwu is the new *juren*, a person who came second in the highest imperial examination. He is not just anybody. He is also a good writer. It is not so easy to pin the young master's murder on him." He shook his head.

The young master heard the hidden message behind the secretary's words, and so, gritting his teeth, he said: "If you can save my life and make that damned Naiwu die in my place, I'll give you another thousand dollars."

Zhao's eyes popped wide with pleasure.

Not to be outdone, Mrs. Liu offered another thousand dollars to make sure her son would be safe and untouched.

Four thousand dollars! Zhao's heart swelled with joy. Smoothing his whiskers he came out with a stratagem. "Since Your Honour, madame and the young master offer me four thousand dollars, this is what we'll do."

The dim light of the Buddhist hall shed a ghostly light on the plotters as they put their heads together. Zhao spoke slowly, emphasizing each word: "The husband was murdered in order to get the wife!"

"The husband was murdered to get the wife," Liu Xitong repeated.

"Thus," said Zhao, "you can make use of this to place one man's blame on another."

As the meaning became clear to him, Liu Zihe clapped his hands with joy.

"In this way Yang Naiwu can take the blame for..."

Turning to her husband, Mrs. Liu said with regret: "For four thousand dollars we get only this?"

Zhao continued outlining the tactics to involve

Naiwu. According to the Qing laws, adultery is proved if the woman confesses. The main stumbling block would be to get her to name Naiwu as her seducer.

"Leave that to me," said Secretary Zhao.

As the explosion of firecrackers sounded in the distance, celebrating the coming nuptials of Yang Naiwu, the conspirators laughed as Zhao remarked: "He will have two happy occasions to celebrate!"

The four broke into sinister laughter.

A lantern moved in the pitch-dark night as two men sneaked out of the side gate of the *yamen* to the prison, from where they secretly took a frightened Xiugu into the inner chamber.

She saw Liu Zihe and tried to retreat, but her way was blocked by the attendant.

Smiling, Liu Zihe walked up and greeted her, his hands held before him: "You have gone through a hard time, Mrs. Ge," he said.

She looked at her tortured hands, all her suffering and rage rose in her like a torrent as she looked at him with hate in her eyes. "I'm sorry I came so late to your rescue," he said.

Xiugu whispered: "You must save my life. Your father is powerful and no-one dares touch the son of the county magistrate."

Liu lied that his father was ignorant of their relationship, so she threatened she would tell the truth in court the next day.

"Put the blame on Naiwu," Liu said. "He had an affair with you. He also wrote out the prescription for your husband. If you accuse him because he harboured designs on you, then we two can be happy together hereafter."

She trembled with rage: "You are a poisonous man, and more worthless than a dog's droppings."

He fell to his knees: "Since we've slept together there must be love between us," he pleaded, "or perhaps you have more feelings for that goat. You must have slept with him too!"

Xiugu struck him across the face.

Now angry, he staggered up and in a fury reminded her of his father's power. "He can make you confess to anything he wants. He can have Sangu and Wenqing's wife sold into prostitution and Yang Naiwu die in prison."

The other three, who had been eavesdropping, emerged from behind the screen. Mrs. Liu could not help but notice what a lovely young thing Xiugu was and how she suited the nickname of Little Cabbage, so elegant yet so pitiable.

Secretary Zhao brought Little Cabbage a cup of tea: "The young master has been teasing you, your mistress. You have nice tender hands, they cannot suffer further torture, can they?"

Xiugu cried out: "A *yamen* represents the government. The official should be just and upright."

He gave a derisive laugh: "The magistrate had your husband's coffin opened and his body examined. Proof was found that Ge Xiaoda died of poisoning. You are accused of murdering your husband. According to the law, you will be cut thirty-six times and bleed to death. Isn't that just?"

Xiugu shuddered as a cold smile played around the corners of the magistrate's mouth.

The secretary went on: "I know you are too kind to want Yang Naiwu exposed. He is after all a new *juren*, and who dares to charge a provincial graduate with murder? His rank exempts him from death. His title may be removed but he can sit for the next imperial examination and become a *juren* again. If you claim that he was the murderer of your husband, he will not be punished and you can clear yourself of the accusation too. But if you claim that our young master is the murderer, he would be sentenced to death since he has no rank. Then the Liu family line ends and your reputation will be sullied as well. You must weigh the matter up and see what is the right thing to do."

Mrs. Liu continued with the pressure: "Who wants to harm Yang Naiwu? He's such a unique man, a man not of the common herd. My husband has the utmost respect for intelligent men like him. Besides, no-one would dare harm a new *juren*. What if the emperor finds out?"

Xiugu replied: "Isn't it true that when a prince breaks the law, even he should be punished just like any other man?"

Zhao broke into laughter: "That is only a smokescreen, young mistress. Haven't you heard of the other saying: 'A magistrate is free to burn down houses while the common people are forbidden even to light a lamp'? All laws protect those above and suppress those down below, ensuring the common people know their place."

"How many princes and lords have you heard of being put to death?" asked Mrs. Liu.

Zhao continued: "Refuse to do what we tell you, and His Honour will be angry. You'll see Ge Wenqing framed as a thief and exiled thousands of miles away, his mother driven out of her home to become a beggar, his wife and your little sister-in-law Sangu sold into prostitution."

Xiugu shuddered as she pictured the ugly scene.

Secretary Zhao, throwing Liu Xitong and his wife a meaningful glance, continued: "Only you can save and protect them, while no harm will befall Mr. Yang. If you don't trust me, don't you trust the county magistrate?"

In answer to Mrs. Liu's summons, a dozen maids filed in with candles lighting up the gloomy hall. They knelt down in front of Xiugu and in one voice chorused: "Young mistress."

Little Cabbage stepped back, flustered and embarrassed.

It was midnight. Secretary Zhao and Liu Xitong were still discussing their tactics. Zhao said doubtfully: "Tomorrow is Yang Naiwu's wedding day. I don't think he will come to court."

Liu Xitong suggested that they send the court runners to arrest him, but Zhao replied that in view of Yang's official rank it couldn't be done. They decided to entice him to the court by deception.

Liu's reprobate son was extremely jealous when he saw how concerned Little Cabbage was about Yang Naiwu. He volunteered to go.

Congratulatory scrolls hung in the hall of the Yang household and red candles were lit to celebrate the coming nuptials of Naiwu. Firecrackers were let off and music blared forth as four men carried his bride in the bright-red and gilded sedan chair to the waiting groom. They bowed to each other while the male guests gathered in the hall celebrating, the women folk and children crowded into the bridal chamber where the bride sat on the edge of the bed with bowed-head. The bed was also in red and gold, and the canopy over the bed was ornately carved.

Eventually two children were chosen to drag Naiwu into the bridal chamber while the rest surrounded him asking for sweetmeats. His sister Shuying told him to ask his bride where they were hidden. More shy than ever, the bride dropped her head even lower.

The children surged towards her clamouring for sweets. As was the custom, the children began to hunt for the wedding goodies until one girl found peanuts and dates below the embroidered pillows. Her mother quickly said: "Those mean that the bride will have a lovely baby soon."

Another child discovered peanuts and pine-nuts in a cupboard inlaid with ivory and the children wrestled with him for a share. At the height of all this hilarity, the servant Chen Laode entered and whispered to Yang Naiwu, who frowned as he followed him out.

Liu Zihe was waiting for him in his study. Their eyes met in mutual hostility, but Naiwu thought to himself: "Enmity is better forgotten than harboured." Besides, it was a happy day for him, so he smiled.

Liu smiled warmly back and greeted Naiwu by folding his hands in front of him: "Congratulations on your wedding day, Mr. Yang. My father has sent me over with a humble gift."

His page-boy put a basket on the desk from which he produced eight gift packages and two rolls of silver dollars wrapped in red paper.

Naiwu protested politely: "I have done nothing to

warrant such a gift from my patron."*

But Liu insisted that he receive the gift, otherwise his father would be hurt.

Reluctantly, Naiwu accepted the gift with grateful thanks.

Liu smiled even more: "Mr. Yang, the Provincial Examiner of Studies has come to the *yamen*. My father wants you to come and discuss a few matters with him."

Naiwu was of course reluctant: "I have many guests tonight and the wedding feast is about to begin."

Liu urged him: "The *yamen* is not very far, it will only take a minute."

He took Naiwu's arm and together they walked to the *yamen* arm-in-arm.

"Two lucky stars are shining over you, Brother Yang — a wedding and an official rank," said Liu with a greasy smile. "Whose help did you get to become a *juren*?"

Naiwu was too disgusted to reply but hurried along so that he could deal with the matters quickly and return to his wedding. He never dreamt that it would be years of hardship and suffering in prison before he would see his home again.

---

*It was the custom for provincial graduates to address the magistrate as his patron.

The Goat Falls into Tiger Jaws

WHEN Yang Naiwu arrived at the *yamen* he saw the magistrate had prepared a feast and he was invited to take the seat of honour. He felt unable to refuse. Liu Xitong, his face wreathed in smiles, said: "Mr. Yang passing the imperial examination has not only brought honour to his family but to all the neighbours and the county *yamen* as well."

Naiwu was anxious to return home and replied he did not deserve such praise and his success was due to his host. "I'm told," he added, "that the Provincial Examiner of Studies has come to discuss matters with me. Where is he?"

Liu Xitong gave a hearty laugh: "There must be a misunderstanding. He has only sent a letter urging all recent graduates to sit the next examination in the capital. I just want to offer you a congratulatory toast."

Naiwu rose to take his leave but he was pulled down as another toast was proffered to celebrate his wedding.

A court runner came in to remind the magistrate he was due in court, but as Naiwu rose to go, Liu persuaded him to wait a little longer as his wife wanted him to take a letter to the capital when he sat for the next examination. He called for two attendants to wait on him while he was away.

The two attendants began to argue because they

wanted to listen in on the court proceedings. Eventually they asked Naiwu if he would accompany them. "It's a very interesting case," they said. "It's about Little Cabbage murdering her husband."

Naiwu was astounded. He could not believe that Xiugu was capable of murdering her husband and was suspicious that there was more to the accusation than met the eye. He rose and accompanied the two attendants to the court room, thus taking the first step towards the trap prepared for him.

The whole scenario had been engineered by Secretary Zhao. Here the saying is true: "An official arena is but a stage." The success of this drama in Yuhang County meant that the magistrate would keep his post, his son save his life and the secretary would make a lot of money; and it all depended now on Little Cabbage's confession.

The vicious plot involved getting Naiwu to a spot where he could see her but she could not see him.

The two attendants took him to the courtyard outside the reception hall where he sat on a stone stool behind a carved wooden balustrade. He could see everything clearly between the gaps but to his surprise, Xiugu kneeling among ferocious court runners did not appear frightened.

Liu Xitong, however, was in a bullying mood. He banged his gavel on the desk and shouted: "What a brazen woman, daring to murder your husband. Who is your adulterer? Confess quickly."

She replied calmly: "There is no adulterer."

He hissed: "If you don't confess you will be tortured." He called for the whip and rattan cane and they were thrown in front of Little Cabbage.

"Will you confess?" he demanded.

"Yes." Xiugu showed no fear.

Naiwu thought it very strange.

Liu Xitong pressed: "Who is the adulterer?"

Hidden behind a screen, Mrs. Liu, Liu Zihe and Secretary Zhao listened with bated breath.

Xiugu answered: "I had a lover before I was married. He was Yang Naiwu."

The two attendants beside Naiwu glanced at him. The colour rose to his cheeks and he felt uneasy.

The listeners behind the screen smiled in relief.

Highly gratified, Secretary Zhao fingered his whiskers. It seemed that the drama he had directed was successful.

But Liu Xitong pretended to be dubious: "Yang Naiwu is a new *juren*. With his status and yours, it is impossible. Don't talk nonsense!"

Xiugu lowered her head and spoke softly: "But it was true."

Liu Xitong pondered for a while: "Did you have anything to do with him after you married Ge Xiaoda?"

"No!"

"Have you really severed all relations?"

"Absolutely!"

Naiwu's nerves barely had time to relax when Xiugu added: "I saw him three times this year."

Naiwu pulled out a handkerchief to wipe the sweat streaming down his face.

"He came to invite us to celebrate his passing the imperial examination and on the third of October he treated my husband's illness. The third time he examined my husband and wrote out a prescription to increase his appetite. The medicine was collected from the pharmacy the same day."

The magistrate pounced on the last piece of information: "What happened after your husband took the medicine?"

Her voice dropped and she began to stutter: "After ... wards ... his eyes, nose, mouth and ears started to bleed that night."

Naiwu went pale. He wondered who had manoeuvered her into making such a confession. To murder the husband in order to get the wife is a crime punishable by death for the man while the woman is allowed to go free.

Behind the screen, Secretary Zhao gave an evil smile.

Torn between contradiction and pain, Xiugu muttered: "Perhaps Mr. Yang made a mistake in his prescription."

Liu Xitong shook his head. "Your husband recovered after the first prescription. The second one was made on the basis of the first. He couldn't have made a mistake."

The magistrate ordered a court officer to search her home for the prescription and then to summon the pharmacist, Qian Baosheng.

Naiwu returned to the waiting room and paced the floor like a restless caged animal while the two attendants kept a close eye on him. When he heard footsteps going past the room towards the reception hall, he wanted to look out but the two men stopped him politely but firmly, saying: "Please have some tea, Mr. Yang."

A court runner entered the room and requested Naiwu to go to the reception hall and see the magistrate.

The hall had been turned into a law court, with Liu Xitong sitting behind the magistrate's desk with court runners on either side. Liu Xitong said: "I have always respected you for your talents, Mr. Yang. As for your morals... I've just had a case a moment ago. The accused Bi Xiugu made a confession. I did not believe her at first. But with witnesses and proof...." He picked up the poem Naiwu had written to Xiugu and the book of accounts from the Benevolent Pharmacy. Your poem says: 'Our ties will last like the ever rolling waters.' What do you have to say?"

Naiwu took the poem and the account book which recorded: "On the seventh of October, Mr. Yang bought arsenic..." He moved forward a step and said: "My patron upholds justice. This is a fraud."

Liu Xitong answered: "I believe you first committed adultery and then not satisfied with that you murdered the husband to get the wife."

Naiwu broke into laughter. "Why don't you catch the real murderer?" he asked. "It's Qian Baosheng."

Liu banged his gavel on his desk again: "Has he had an affair with Xiugu?"

"I don't know," answered Naiwu.

Feeling justice was on his side, Naiwu replied with confidence that he had been in Hangzhou on the date mentioned in the book of accounts and had not returned home until the tenth. "How could I have purchased poison from the Benevolent Pharmacy? Ask the one who put that item down, he must know who the culprit is."

Liu Xitong was silenced for a while digesting the sharpness of Naiwu's words. Then he ordered that

Qian Baosheng should be brought before the court.

Qian knelt before the magistrate as he was accused of lying. He shouted at Naiwu: "Mr. Yang, you bought arsenic from my pharmacy on the seventh. You can't deny it!"

Naiwu was stung to retort: "Don't be greedy for small gains. Truth will be out sooner or later. Don't you know the relationship between 'gains and losses'?"

Qian was silent as his evil eyes darted round the courtroom.

Liu Xitong, feeling he was losing control, asked: "Was there a feud between you and Ge Xiaoda?"

Qian answered: "None in this life or in a previous one."

Liu then asked him: "Why did you murder him?"

"I should be asking that question, Your Honour, please look at the account book."

Liu Xitong read out aloud: "On the seventh of October, Mr. Yang Naiwu bought three *qian**.

Liu Xitong sneered: "What more do you have to say now before the witness and the proof, Mr. Yang Naiwu?"

Naiwu answered bitterly: "Witness and proof? You certainly know what this is all about!"

Liu Xitong became hostile. "You claim I am the instigator of these confessions? I am not like you, always writing complaints for tricky persons and who gathers crowds and makes trouble. I won't let you off easily."

"So," said Naiwu, "you are avenging yourself for

---

*A unit of five grams.

being thrown out of office at the Canqian granary."

Liu Xitong flew into a rage: "Take him away and have him flogged!"

"Who dares to do that?" Naiwu challenged.

The court runners were too frightened to approach him.

The chief of the court runners walked forward and bowed: "He has a title, Your Honour."

"So what?" Liu demanded: "In three days, I'll report to the Provincial Examiner of Studies and have his title removed."

At Yang Naiwu's home the tables were laden with food and wine and the guests sat waiting for his return, but time went by and they began to get uneasy. Yang's best friends, Shi, Kong and Li, suggested to his sister, Shuying, that they should start without him. The bride entered the hall. She had taken off her crimson wedding dress and had changed into another embroidered red dress. She sat alone at the table, not eating anything. The three friends toasted the bride and she modestly lowered her head.

Meanwhile Naiwu was still detained in the hall of the Confucian Temple with the two court runners keeping watch. His feelings were mixed, not too worried because of his status, but this was his wedding day and he and his bride were apart. He looked out of the window and saw that the moon was covered by heavy clouds and the night seemed ominously darker than usual.

The banquet in his home had ended some time ago and all the lights were out.

In the bridal chamber, wax dripped down like tears from a pair of red candles. Naiwu's sister sat with the dejected bride. She was still in her wedding clothes. Shuying tried to console her but it only made her more unhappy as she wondered what had happened to her husband. As night deepened the candles flickered and went out. The moon emerged from the thick clouds and shed its light on the tearful waiting bride.

Three days later, Naiwu was once again taken to the *yamen* where the magistrate sat arrogantly at his desk and the court runners seemed to be more ferocious and intimidating than ever.

Naiwu was calm and composed despite the threatening noises the court runners made.

Liu Xitong was infuriated by his calm demeanour and sneered: "You think you still have a title, and dare to address me as your patron?" He ordered his clerk to read out an order from the Provincial Literary Chancellor.

"According to the magistrate of Yuhang County, the new *juren* Yang Naiwu wrote letters on behalf of dissidents, conducted disorderly behaviour in the court, murdered the husband of a woman in order to possess her. His title is now removed so that he can be tried for these crimes and investigation and punishment can be carried out."

Naiwu felt his head would burst. He had studied since he was seven years old to achieve his title of *juren* at the age of 25. Now his title had been taken away in the short space of three days. Overcome with untold sadness, he said: "I can see the might of your influence, patron."

Sneering, Liu Xitong snapped: "Not necessarily. Get down on your knees now!"

Naiwu thought: "I mustn't kneel. If I do not confess when he interrogates me, he is sure to use torture. I can't allow him to do it here. He must do it in the big hall so that people can see I have been unjustly accused.'' He remained standing, head raised and asked: "Will Your Honour tell me where this is?"

"The reception hall of the *yamen*."

"What is a reception hall used for?"

"A reception hall...?" Liu Xitong didn't know what to say.

"A reception hall is part of the private quarters of the *yamen* and is not a place for a criminal to bend his his knees," Naiwu said. "The Qing Government's law stipulates that no illegal courts are to be held. To be interrogated in the reception hall is illegal."

Liu Xitong was shamed and snapped out the order for the court to be moved to the middle hall.

The court runners thought it strange. It was usually the magistrate who questioned the accused, not the other way round.

The middle hall was quickly turned into a courtroom.

Again Liu Xitong took up his position as the magistrate. The court runners ordered Naiwu to kneel down, but he still refused.

"Is this the middle hall?" he asked.

"A middle hall is a middle hall and that is that!" snarled Liu Xitong.

Naiwu laughed derisively. "You don't know because you bought your post. The middle hall is between the principal hall and the inner quarters. It separates the public and the private quarters. Holding court here is neither public nor private. I would rather you do this publicly."

The magistrate clenched his teeth and gave the order to move the court to the principal hall. The court runners were called back from the opium dens and teahouses, putting on their uniforms as they ran to their posts. The sound of the drum and the gong reverberated throughout the area as the gate of the *yamen* was flung wide open. People crowded in to hear the case. The court runner in charge of torture brought out whips and rattan canes, and other instruments. In a charcoal brazier, an iron chain became red-hot.

Yang's good friends, Kong and Li, accompanied by his faithful servant Chen Laode, were among the audience. In the hall hung notices with the words: "Silence", "Withdraw", "Magistrate of Yuhang County" and "Official of the Seventh Grade".

Things were different this time. With no status to protect him, Naiwu was tortured. Rods squeezed his legs to breaking point, and pain shot through his body. He screamed and lost consciousness. A feeling of satisfaction and revenge surged through Liu Xitong as he saw his victim in pain. A ladle of cold water was poured on Naiwu's face but he remained unconscious. A bowl of vinegar was brought and a hot coal dropped in; the stringent smoke was held under his nose. Slowly he opened his eyes and as they focussed on the posters which read "Silence", "Withdraw", and then another notice which read: "Be Sharp-eyed and Hold Justice. He asked for Xiugu to be brought in.

Even in prison clothes, her beauty was striking. She was heartbroken when she saw the once handsome

Naiwu haggard and dishevelled. Secretary Zhao had tricked her and now, as regret burning within her, she was also frightened.

Pointing at Naiwu, Liu Xitong demanded: "Is this your adulterer?"

She did not answer.

Prostrate on the floor, Naiwu raised his head and looked at her. There was no reproach in his eyes, only sadness and hope.

Kneeling, she tried to reach him but the court runners prevented her. Naiwu spoke with difficulty: "Xiugu, you must know what kind of man I am, how I have behaved to you and your husband. Now in this law court, before everybody, please tell the truth."

Liu Xitong banged his gavel: "The law is relentless. Tell nothing but the truth, otherwise you had better watch out. Watch out!" Xiugu wept but couldn't speak.

Naiwu stared at Xiugu as he pleaded: "Did I murder your husband?"

She moved her lips....

Naiwu waited tense and expectant. The onlookers watched her breathlessly as they waited for her to point out the murderer of her husband.

A Sinister Hand Blocks the Sky

"YOUR Honour," Xiugu faltered, "Yang Naiwu is wr..."

Naiwu's eyes lit up with hope as soon as she began "wr..." but Liu Xitong quickly butted in: "Wrong? I know he is in the wrong to get you by killing your husband. Take her away."

As the court runners pulled the protesting Xiugu away, the magistrate, white-faced with anger, shouted at Naiwu: "You have seen her. Now own up quickly."

Naiwu dusted his clothes and retorted: "As a high official and the magistrate of Yuhang, are you sure you didn't misunderstand what Xiugu said?"

"She said you were the wrong person to have loved."

"No!" Naiwu said firmly. "She claimed that I was wronged."

"Rubbish!" retorted Liu Xitong.

Naiwu answered: "Then you are not a magistrate who works for the people but someone who rides roughshod over them."

Liu Xitong slammed his gavel on the desk and called for the red-hot chain.

Two pairs of pincers picked up the chain from the brazier and tossed it onto the tiled floor and then it was pulled straight.

Naiwu's friends, Shi, Kong and Li, could stay silent no longer. They rose and bowed before the magistrate.

Shi began: "Our patron has always been a benevolent man and loves the people like his own sons. The use of so many severe tortures today will cast a shadow over your good name."

Liu Xitong answered equally politely: "Normally I do not want a confession through the use of torture. But Yang Naiwu is too evil and cunning. He would never confess unless torture is used."

Kong asked: "Do you have proof of his crime, patron?"

Liu repeated the evidence of the account book of the Benevolent Pharmacy.

Kong said: "That is very strange. On the seventh of October, Yang Naiwu was in Hangzhou with us. We did not return until the tenth."

The magistrate was stunned for a moment, but as things had gone so far he could only grasp at straws. He insisted that on that date Naiwu had been drinking at his place.

Kong was angry and burst out: "Ridiculous. Could there be two Yang Naiwus? There is no justice here. Many people in power seem to put their own interests first. One day the truth will be out and it will be too late for you to repent, patron."

Liu Xitong took off his official hat and placed it on the desk. "I only need to knock over my desk to have you charged with trouble-making in the court. Now, all of you go!"

They did not budge.

He gave an evil smile and ordered the chain to be prepared.

Naiwu was pulled over to the hot chain.

"Will you confess?" Liu demanded.

Naiwu gritted his teeth and closed his eyes. He didn't care any more.

"Put him on it," ordered Liu.

This punishment was capable of crippling a man for life and was only used on diehard robbers. The court runners hesitated. But Liu Xitong had gone too far to draw back. He patted his chest meaning that he would be responsible for the results and cried: "Put him on it! Put him on it!"

Black smoke rose and flesh sizzled. Naiwu lost consciousness.

His friend Kong, tears streaming from his eyes, said: "You have suffered dreadfully, Brother Naiwu. We'll appeal to a higher *yamen*."

Hearing this, Liu knocked over his desk and yelled: "How dare you are! Making trouble in court!"

Naiwu, who had never dreamed that he would be transformed from a respected *juren* into a criminal and end up in jail instead of his wedding chamber, regained consciousness. He realized that only now that he had been badly tortured and was being forced to make a false confession under duress could he complain to a higher court.

He was given a piece of paper and ordered to write his confession.

Doubled up in pain he wrote: "In order to get the wife, I murdered the husband. Now that I have murdered the husband, I can get the wife." And then with a trembling hand he signed.

"Take him to prison," ordered the triumphant Liu Xitong.

A drum was beaten and a gong struck as slowly the *yamen* closed its gate.

His body covered in blood and his ankles in heavy chains, Naiwu was thrown onto the damp floor of a dark cell.

He opened his eyes and looked at his surroundings. Wood railings formed one wall while the other three sides were bricks with a small skylight which let in a streak of light.

Several prisoners with dirty faces and uncombed hair gazed at him.

One prisoner laughed sarcastically as he addressed Naiwu as "Mr. *juren*".

A warder looked in and snapped: "There's no *juren* in prison, only criminals."

Naiwu noticed a prisoner hanging from a beam by his pigtail and the warder called out: "There's good dramatic scene for you too!"

Another prisoner crawled over to him and said: "If a new prisoner does not present gifts to the warder, he will be...."

Naiwu stared at the scene before him and shuddered.

When the Yang's family retainer, Chen Laode, returned home from the *yamen* he recounted to Naiwu's sister Shuying all that had happened. Colour drained from her face and Naiwu's young bride broke down and wailed. The whole household cried except Shuying.

"Don't worry," she consoled her sister-in-law. "This is because the magistrate harbours a grudge against Naiwu. I will try to clear his name as long as there is breath in me."

Just then Naiwu's friends, Shi, Kong and Li,

called. As soon as they sat down, they said that they intended to file a complaint to a higher level.

Shuying was worried that their involvement might affect their futures, but they insisted that Naiwu's good name was more important.

"Brother Yang has spent ten hard years studying for the imperial examination," said Li. "It's outrageous that a magistrate should torture him to force a false confession."

Kong was equally incensed that a state which claimed to set a high store by its intellectuals should disgrace them by such means.

But Shuying refused their offers of help, saying: "It's the duty of our family to save him. I can never allow outsiders to be involved."

"He is like a brother to us, Miss Yang..." they protested, but Shuying cut them short: "We have to kill two birds with one stone and not to kill one bird with two stones. If you appeal to a higher court my brother could still lose his life and you your future careers. Mr. Kong has passed the provincial examination and in a few days is due to take his finals in the capital. If you miss the exam that will affect your future. Then who could put in a word for him? Once the document arrives at Yuhang from the capital, my brother would be beheaded. Isn't that killing one bird with two stones?"

Shi still did not understand Shuying's reference to killing two birds with one stone. So she explained: "Your father is on good terms with Mr. Xia, the vice-president of the Board of Punishment. If you could take a letter to him from your father when you are in the capital asking him to intervene, it might help

Naiwu's case as Mr. Xia's words carry weight. Then your future is not affected and Naiwu could be saved. Isn't that killing two birds with one stone?"

Shi answered: "Miss Yang is really an outstanding woman, a far cry from the likes of us."

Kong sighed sadly: "I didn't think I would have to go to the capital without Brother Yang. What a pity!"

Shuying bowed: "It is times like these when a person is in trouble that people drop stones on a fallen man or look on with folded arms. I am most grateful to you gentlemen for standing up to help him." She bowed deeply to them. They bowed back in return.

When they had left, Shuying, accompanied by the family retainer, Chen Laode, went to the prison. She had not expected to see her brother so injured and in chains so soon after leaving home. She could no longer hold back her tears.

To ease her mind, Naiwu put on a cheerful face and said jokingly in a hoarse voice: "This cell is not bad. It only costs five silver dollars a day."

Shuying badly wanted to know the truth — whether he and Xiugu had really been lovers — but he cut her off in mid-sentence. "It all happened two years ago and then I stopped seeing her. Do you suspect me like the others too? I am just worried that evil magistrate will have me killed before I have had a chance to write a statement to clear myself."

"Do it right away," said Shuying, "I'll go to the prefectural *yamen* tomorrow."

In the dust-speckled light that came from the narrow window, Shuying knelt down so that her brother could use her back as a table to write his statement.

The Hangzhou *yamen* was situated beside the enchanting West Lake. A tall flagpole stood before its double-eaved roof.

Secretary Liu was reading the complaint sent in by Shuying as well as the report from the Yuhang County Court.

Secretary Liu, in his fifties, was an upright man. He was tall and slim and dressed simply in a cap and a gown of blue cloth. Frowning, he pounded the desk in anger as he shouted: "This is outrageous!"

The Prefect of Hangzhou, Chen Lu, stepped in.

Pointing at the report sent by the Yuhang County Court, the Secretary said: "This is absolute rubbish!"

Chen answered: "We had a heated debate yesterday on this case. I think they are guilty." He patted his fat stomach complacently. But the secretary rejoined: "Do you consider Yang Naiwu a clever man or a stupid one?"

"He is doubtlessly a clever man."

"Then why should he do such a stupid thing?"

The complacent smile disappeared from Chen's face.

Secretary Liu went on: "Two years ago, when Little Cabbage was even younger and more beautiful and Yang Naiwu was a mere scholar, they did not conspire together, and when he became a *juren*, why should they conspire then? Does that make sense?"

But Chen was adamant: "Compared to a mere scholar, a *juren* has a higher status and carries more weight. He wouldn't bother about murdering a lowly beancurd seller. Yes, people with status and weight carry themselves well."

"Not necessarily," said Secretary Liu. "An official has power. Evil-doers are usually county magistrates and prefects. They have power and influence."

Secretary Liu then picked up Shuying's petition: "What about this then?"

"Because of what you've said, I'll accept it," said Chen. "Please order the prisoners to be brought here immediately. If it is a murder case, they could be executed."

It was the middle of the night. In the men's cells of Yuhang Prison, a warder knelt down before a picture of Lord Xiao* and kowtowed three times, muttering: "I am only carrying our orders. It has really nothing to do with me."

He downed a bowl of spirits to give himself courage.

A pale melancholy moon shone on the high prison walls, and over the trees swaying in a cold breeze. Fallen leaves fluttered down accompanied by the doleful sound of "duo, duo, duo," as the night-watchman beat his drum. It was the second watch. Chained hand and foot, Naiwu heard footsteps outside his cell and saw the warder come in with a lantern in one hand and a wine bottle and sandbag in the other.

"Congratulations, Mr. Yang," said the warder.

Naiwu realized what was going to happen and almost fainted.

"Someone wants you dead badly, not me. I'm only doing as I'm told," said the warder.

---

*It was believed that Xiao He, a prime minister of the Western Han Dynasty was the creator of Chinese criminal law. Therefore in prisons, a "Xiao He Hall" was usually set up with his portrait.

A Sinister Hand Blocks the Sky 93

He offered him the wine. "Drink. It will make it easier."

Naiwu knew that pleading for his life would be useless, so he had better get drunk and die quickly. He grabbed the wine, looked round at his surroundings and sighed: "I began my studies when I was six years old and only became a *juren* recently. Who would have thought that I would be falsely accused and die in prison?" He tossed back his head and gulped down half a bottle, but the alcohol cleared his head instead of befuddling him and he cried out: "Oh heaven. Why did I bother to study? What's the use of being a *juren*? Is there any law or justice?"

"It's late, Mr. Yang," said the warder. "Drunk or not, you're going to die." He was eager to finish the job and claim his reward. Naiwu dashed the wine bottle to the ground and broke into wild laughter.

The warder felt goose pimples rising on his body.

"How many times can one laugh with such abandonment in one's life? Have I been born into this world just to meet this end?" Naiwu knelt down and kowtowed to his ancestors. "I'm an unfilial son. Please forgive me." Then he lay down on the ground and stretched out his legs. "I'll settle accounts with you when I'm dead, Liu Xitong," he said and waited for death. The warder knelt down and pressed the sandbag on Naiwu's nose and mouth.

Suddenly torches appeared and a court runner cried: "The Hangzhou *yamen* is here to bring the criminal under their jurisdiction."

The warder jumped like a scalded cat and scampered off. Yang Naiwu's face was drained of colour and there seemed to be no breath left in him.

Meanwhile in the home of the architect of Naiwu's misfortunes, Secretary Zhao was gloating over the piles of silver dollars given to him by the magistrate's family. His windows and doors were closed and he had placed a statue of the God of Wealth riding on a black tiger with whip in hand before him. Four thousand dollars! Zhao sipped some wine, tossed a peanut into his mouth and picked up a piece of beef with his chopsticks. His heart was bursting with happiness, as he hummed a line from a Peking opera: "I, the emperor, is drunk in the peach blossom palace..."

Someone hammered on the door. He put down his wine-cup and placing his arms round the silver dollars, shouted out: "Who is it?"

"The magistrate wants to see you, Mr. Zhao."

Before he had even sat down, Mrs. Liu said in a panic: "Things look very bad. The Hangzhou *yamen* has sent for Yang Naiwu and Little Cabbage."

Liu Xitong added: "I followed your advice to have Yang Naiwu killed but I didn't anticipate the Hangzhou *yamen* would act so quickly."

Zhao said: "Let them be taken away."

Mrs. Liu screeched: "Are you crazy? What if the prefectural *yamen* finds out the truth? Remember, it was your idea to have Yang Naiwu shoulder the blame for my son."

Zhao fingered his goatee and said: "But isn't the prefect of Hangzhou related to you by marriage?"

"In a murder case, I don't think he'll take that into account," said Liu Xitong.

Zhao suggested that the magistrate visit the prefect and take him an expensive present.

Liu Xitong was not convinced: "He has a good reputation. If he should refuse?..."

"It all depends on what kind of gift you're giving him and how you give it," said Zhao.

Mrs. Liu agreed: "All officials are greedy."

Liu Xitong still remained uneasy: "But what if Yang Naiwu complains to an even higher *yamen*. I would have wasted all my property for nothing."

Zhao reassured him that by involving his direct superior, the latter would carry the responsibility if Naiwu was successful in petitioning the authorities at provincial level.

Liu Xitong relaxed but Zhao warned that they had convinced Little Cabbage that Yang Naiwu would only have his title removed and would not be executed. If she subsequently found out the truth, she would not be able to keep quiet.

Zhao assured them that as he had taken their money he would think out a plan. With that he whispered in their ears.

Within the cold water chamber of the prison, a girl's frightened shrieks were heard. "I want to go home! I want to go home!" The cry made Xiugu look out and she saw behind the wooden railing a terrified Sangu beating at the water trying to drive away water snakes. Her face was bleeding and her hair in tangles.

When she heard Xiugu call to her, she struggled over to the wooden rails and held on with all her might. "Help me, sister-in-law!" she cried.

Secretary Zhao appeared beside the prison door: "She could be set free if you give a promise."

Xiugu hung her head as she realized she was powerless to protest.

Zhao grabbed Sangu's pigtail and pushed the screaming child into the dirty water. "Promise you stick to what you confessed before," he snarled at Xiugu.

As Sangu's struggles grew weaker, Xiugu had no choice but to agree to cooperate. "Let her go!" she said.

No Reverse of Verdict

MRS. Liu, the magistrate's wife, took Xiugu to a room in the inner quarters of the *yamen*. On the table, in a lacquer box traced with designs of gold were two deer antlers, an enormous pearl brooch and a gold statue of the God of Longevity. Picking up the brooch, Mrs. Liu boasted: "This is made with six hundred pearls and is going as a present to the favourite fifth concubine of the prefect. As a matter of fact his daughter is married to my nephew. Our two families are related by marriage. Yang Naiwu will have nothing to worry about. The removal of his title was his only punishment but now he has lodged a complaint at the prefectural *yamen*, he should know nothing will come of it."

Xiugu was silent, her eyes leveled ahead.

With a wave of her hand, Xiugu was led away. Mrs. Liu went into the next room where her husband had been eavesdropping and told him: "Now you can set your heart at ease."

Liu Xitong made for the main hall and ordered Naiwu to be brought in. The threshold was too high for him to lift his badly wounded legs over it, so the court runners unceremoniously dragged him in.

Liu Xitong looked at the shackled man in prison garb. "You have confessed to killing the husband in order to get the wife. Why then have you told your family to lodge a complaint at the Hangzhou *yamen*?"

Naiwu answered: "Because there is no justice here." Looking at the placard "Be Sharp-eyed and Hold Justice" hanging on the wall, he added confidently: "I will be cleared there."

Liu Xitong snarled: "Your punishment will be doubly severe."

Naiwu answered: "I'm supposed to be executed in the autumn. Are you planning to chop off my head more than once?"

Liu Xitong said: "You would have been better off if the case had been handled locally because when there is an amnesty I could have given you a pardon. Although people in my jurisdiction are jailed for their crimes, their sentences can be reduced provided they have behaved themselves. Think it over and see which will benefit you the most. To admit your crime here and serve your sentence or lodge a complaint at a higher level. It is never too late to repent."

Naiwu retorted: "Do you mean that the prefect of Hangzhou also embezzles villagers' grain and breaks the law?"

Liu Xitong threw down a bamboo slip which ordered the prisoner to be taken to another place: "Take him to Hangzhou tomorrow morning," he said angrily and adjourned the court.

The following morning Xiugu was disturbed from her reverie by the clang of the iron door to her cell and the wardress ordering her out.

She trembled at the thought of what was in store for her. Another interrogation?

But a guard came and snapped: "Be quick! Don't dawdle. You're moving to the court of the Hangzhou

Prefecture."

The strong sunlight made her blink and passers-by pointed and sneered at her: "Look, there is Little Cabbage!"

"Killing her husband. What a vicious woman!"

She was taken to the water front where she saw a *yamen* boat waiting for her. Yang Naiwu was already sitting in the stern.

As they stared at each other they wondered what kind of fate awaited them.

Dismal clouds floated above and the river swept past. The two pagodas representing male and female stood on the hill, a mute example of its unchanging environment, unlike the changes of the ill-starred sweethearts. This was where she had first met Naiwu before she was married. Then, willow branches swayed, light smoke rose from cooking stoves and butterflies darted in pairs and the water below the Stone Lion Bridge was so clear that one could see the bottom of the riverbed.

She remembered the time when she was slowly walking up the steps to the bridgehead with her basket of washed vegetables, and finding her way blocked by a familiar figure. She looked up and saw a purse she had embroidered hanging from his waist and then the handsome face of Naiwu.

Heavily shackled, they were kept at opposite ends of the boat as it left on its journey to Hangzhou. She was overcome — the scenery was the same, but things had changed.

Chen Lu, the prefect of Hangzhou, and Liu Zhaoji, secretary of the Hangzhou *yamen*, were drinking in a pavilion at the edge of a pond in the back garden of the Hangzhou *yamen*.

Chen Lu sipped some wine, then with his silver chopsticks picked up a live shrimp with its whiskers and feelers cut off, dipped it into some sesame sauce and popped it into his big mouth.

"I like live shrimp best," he said to Liu and gestured to him to help himself.

Liu shook his head: "No, I'm not brave enough to eat shrimps that way."

Chen Lu guffawed. Pointing at him with his silver chopsticks he said: "You have the heart of Buddha. By the way, Yang Naiwu and other criminals have arrived in Hangzhou. How should we go about it?"

"I think the case can be solved with just one interrogation. We need only question one person, and that is the young proprietor of the pharmacy, Qian Baosheng."

"Is he the adulterer?"

"No," answered Liu. "On the date in question Yang Naiwu was in Hangzhou. The one who wrote down the false entry in the account book must either be the murderer or an accomplice. And I believe the murderer is either the nephew or the son of the Yuhang magistrate."

Chen looked at Liu in admiration: "It seems you're not just a secretary but a living god!"

Liu answered: "I have just reasoned it out."

Chen said: "If that is the case, the Yuhang magistrate is very stupid!"

Liu warned Chen to be careful in handling this case since Chen himself was related by marriage to the magistrate.

Chen answered: "He will come if he has not wronged Yang Naiwu, otherwise he would not dare to see me."

Liu smiled: "I think he would come even if he is guilty. Besides, he would even bring you a large gift."

Just at that moment the servant announced the presense of the magistrate of Yuhang County.

Prefect Chen pulled a long face and refused to see him.

The attendant whispered in his ear and Chen asked what clothes he was wearing.

"Black clothes and a cap*," came the answer. "Then I'll see him in the study," said Chen.

Secretary Liu reminded him as he got up: "Arsenic mixed with honey is sweet to the taste but kills just the same, sir."

"A hundred taels of gold cannot move me," Chen said and threw down his silver chopsticks.

Live shrimps hopped on the plate. Liu picked them up and dropped them into the pond.

Without feelers the shrimps drew up their bodies and slowly sank to the bottom, unable to swim.

There are three kinds of officials: one who wants a reputation and to whom money is unimportant, the second wants both reputation and money and the third wants money only and cares nothing about reputation. To which category did the prefect of Hangzhou belong?

Before seeing the Yuhang magistrate, Chen Lu put on his official dress and cap, because official rites in the Qing Dynasty were very strict. It was considered a

---

*Black clothing was worn by court runners and police in the Qing Dynasty.

crime to see one's inferior in private without wearing official dress. The prefect of Hangzhou intended to intimidate the Yuhang magistrate with his official dress, so that he would be unable to ask for personal favours.

As Liu Xitong entered the study he drew in his breath when he saw his relative by marriage sitting cold and straight-backed in official dress. He signalled to the pageboy carrying the gifts not to follow him in and greeted the prefect with obsequious smiles. With a solemn face, Chen demanded: "Who are you?"

Liu Xitong walked up a step and made a deep bow: "Your subordinate, the magistrate of Yuhang, is paying his respects to Your Honour."

Chen appeared not to see or hear him.

Once again Liu Xitong bowed.

"Are you the magistrate of Yuhang?" Chen asked finally.

"Yes sir."

"Then what kind of official dress are you wearing that you dare claim to be the magistrate of Yuhang?"

"Your subordinate's official dress is in the boat. I did not dare put it on because I have come to see Your Honour on an important matter," the magistrate answered.

"Do you realize you have broken etiquette by coming to the *yamen* and seeing your superior in private?" Chen picked up his teacup and his attendant cried: "See the guest out!"

Although the magistrate of Yuhang met with a rebuff, he was nevertheless an old hand in official circles. Deciding to avoid direct contact he adopted roundabout tactics by calling upon Chen Lu's favourite Fifth Concubine. In her scented luxurious boudoir the young coquette was placing the huge pearl brooch against her breast and smiling. Liu Xitong was quick with his flattery: "That pearl brooch highlights your complexion. Words cannot describe the outstanding match of these pearls with your flawless beauty."

Hating to part with the brooch, Fifth Concubine inquired coyly: "How much did it cost, sir?"

"This is a small token for your birthday," he said and the pageboy presented her with the two antlers and the statue of the God of Longevity in pure gold.

"Oh so many valuable gifts!" she protested. "Why do I deserve such precious gifts?"

"I hope you will put in a good word for me with your husband," Liu Xitong said.

Fifth Concubine gave him a sweet smile.

That evening as Chen Lu rocked himself in his chair, Fifth Concubine placed the pearl brooch on her breast and said to him: "Isn't it beautiful?" She brought out the antlers and the gold statue. "I've always wanted a pearl brooch. You've made many promises but never bought one for me." She added demurely: "These antlers will build up your health. What do you think the statue weighs?"

"Has the Yuhang magistrate been visiting?" Chen asked suspiciously.

"What does it matter who gave them?" she replied.

"We can't accept," the prefect was quite adamant.

Fifth Concubine stamped her foot and widened her eyes in a glare until they looked like apricots. "You don't buy them for me and when someone else gives them to me, you won't let me have them. You do not love me at all. Go away! I don't want you here!"

Her anger only made her more attractive and desirable.

Chen laughed and said: "Alright. I'll overlook it."

She said petulantly: "But I want you to look into this affair. He is waiting for you in the tea-drinking hall."

As Prefect Chen strode in Liu Xitong moved forward and bowed.

"You've come to present birthday gifts?" Chen asked.

Liu nodded.

"Aha! We're related by marriage."

They discussed the case of Yang Naiwu and Liu Xitong expressed his concern that the verdict might be overturned.

"Rest assured," said Chen. "It would be better if we go to see my secretary first."

Taking the hint, Liu Xitong handed him a cheque.

Secretary Liu Zhaoji was reading in his office when he saw the prefect and the magistrate chatting amiably as they headed in his direction. He mumbled to himself: "When a man becomes an official, he changes. He forgets his conscience and takes bribes." Ignoring their entrance he went on reading.

Only when the prefect tapped him on the shoulder did he raise his eyes and look at him.

Pretending to be surprised he asked: "Aren't you the magistrate of Yuhang County? Why have you condescended to come to this tiny study?"

With an oily smile, Liu Xitong said: "I've specially come to see you."

The prefect interrupted: "The Yuhang magistrate has come to see you on the one hand but on the other he has some official business to discuss with you."

Liu Zhaoji answered: "In that case he should discuss it with the secretary in his own *yamen*."

"It concerns the Yang Naiwu case," said Chen.

His secretary replied: "The less reason for him to come to this prefectural *yamen*."

"Yang Naiwu is a bad character," said Chen.

Liu Zhaoji challenged him. "How do you know that before you have interrogated him?"

Liu Xitong butted in: "I have already gone through the case. He is guilty of murder. We cannot allow him to reverse the verdict here."

Liu Zhaoji answered that the simple solution would be to chop off his head before he opened his mouth.

The prefect took out a money order for three hundred dollars from his sleeve, saying: "The Yuhang magistrate is giving you this to buy some tonic for your health."

Liu Zhaoji was overwhelmed and took the money order but then said: "How come the money the Yuhang magistrate gives me comes out of your sleeve? A gentleman loves money but he acquires it in a proper way. He may be poor, but his will-power is never poor. I won't accept it. There are nine counties below the Hangzhou prefecture, and the county magistrates follow the example of the prefect. If the prefect is not corrupt, the nine magistrates are not greedy. If the prefect is corrupt, the magistrates will break the law willy-nilly. A drop of wine in official circles amounts to a thousand drops of blood of the people. Money is good but heavenly justice is formidable. I think it is not Yang Naiwu who should be tried for murder but someone in your *yamen*. I am not interested in money," and he returned the cheque.

Liu Xitong's face went white but Chen burst out laughing. Then he asked his secretary: "Are you related to Yang Naiwu then?"

Liu Zhaoji was indignant and his beard quivered. "He is not related to me nor are we friends. I don't even know the man."

Waving the cheque, Chen answered: "I was only testing you with this."

As his meaning dawned on Liu Zhaoji, he still hoped the prefect would not be influenced by the fact he was related to the magistrate. He said: "I hope you will act with justice tomorrow."

Seeing the consternation of the Yuhang magistrate made Liu Zhaoji feel better. He held his hands together in front of him and bowed before leaving.

Liu Xitong was worried: "Tomorrow, when interrogating Yang Naiwu ... you must not let him reverse the verdict. My position is at stake and my life and family...."

Chen touched his official cap thoughtfully.

Would Secretary Liu's sudden retreat have an effect on the conscience of the prefect of Hangzhou who had been upright until now?

The results could only be seen the following morning in court.

Re-examination in Hangzhou

GUARDS stood on both sides of the tall and imposing gate of the *yamen* of the Hangzhou prefecture as the townspeople gathered round and read the notice emblazoned with a tiger's head which announced the re-examination of Yang Naiwu's case. Suddenly the gate was thrown open to the sound of gongs and drums as the prisoner, wearing a cangue and in a wooden cage, was carried out by the court runners. The people surged forward to take a closer look. Some spat or threw stones at him.

"A shameless scoundrel!"

"A wicked man who murdered the husband to get the wife. And a *juren* too!"

"He ought to be cut into a thousand pieces."

"Evil-doers will come to a bad end. Heaven is just."

Naiwu closed his eyes to shut out the scene.

Shuying pushed her way through the crowds and called to him. Her voice made him open his eyes and he moved his lips but no sound came. She clutched the bars of the cage. "We're pinning our hopes on your life being saved," she said. "Take care what you say."

His eyes aglow, he said: "Don't worry, sister, I suffered all the cruel tortures at Yuhang so that I could come to this court."

The gate of the *yamen*, looking like the entrance to a temple, was wide open as people streamed into the main hall and stood behind the wooden balustrades. Police and court runners stood on both sides, each looking fiercer than the other.

Prefect Chen Lu, in his official clothes and hat, sat majestically at his desk. Yang Naiwu, though dirty and dishevelled, felt confident as he knelt before him. The prefect looked sternly at him and inquired: "Are you the new graduate who won the title of Filial Piety and Uprightness?" Picking up a piece of paper, he added: "Is this a love poem you wrote to Xiugu?"

Chen was intimidating from the start: "You seduced a childbride, harming the body your parents gave you. Where is your filial piety? Where is your uprightness?"

Sitting on an elevated platform, Liu Xitong was overjoyed, so set was he to have Naiwu executed and thus to protect his life and family.

But on the other side of a screen, Chen's secretary, Liu Zhaoji, frowned, still hoping that the prefect would be fair and just. Naiwu spoke: "I have cut off all relations with Xiugu a long time ago and I have nothing to do with her husband's death."

"It says here in your own handwriting: 'Our ties will last like the ever rolling waters'. How can you claim to have cut off all relations with her?" Before Naiwu could answer, Chen continued: "When Ge Xiaoda fell ill, was it you who made out the prescription for him?"

Naiwu had to admit that he had written the prescription but added: "If I had wanted to kill him I could have made out a prescription to accelerate his disease instead of curing him. Then he would have died as a result of a quack medicine. I wouldn't have needed poison."

Chen picked up the account book and asked if he had gone to the pharmacy to get arsenic on the seventh of October.

Yang Naiwu once again repeated he had not been in Yuhang on that date and it was a wrong entry.

In the background, Liu Zhaoji nodded his head, the facts were beginning to be clear.

As Naiwu was questioned further and the facts emerged that he had been tortured into making a false confession, Chen said: "If you have been falsely accused I will clear your name."

Naiwu kowtowed again and again in relief, saying: "You are an upright judge. Your name will last for ever."

Relief also showed on Liu Zhaoji's face but the magistrate, Liu Xitong, was full of misgivings.

At the side door, Fifth Concubine waved her handkerchief at Chen Lu as he walked during a recess. "What is the matter with you?" she demanded.

Returning to his armchair, he closed his eyes and said nothing.

Fifth Concubine wiped his brow and beard with a hot towel. "Are you going to clear him?" she asked.

He replied: "It's none of your business. You're a woman, return to your room."

Fifth Concubine stamped her foot, and as she left gave him a hard look.

Chen took a pinch from his snuff bottle, returned to court and ordered that Little Cabbage — Xiugu — be brought in. Despite her prison ordeal, she was still strikingly beautiful and for a while he forgot where he was as he gazed at her. Then collecting himself he asked: "Did you have an affair with Yang Naiwu and was your husband murdered by him?"

Xiugu's lips moved but no sound came.

"Speak," he cried.

The picture of her young sister-in-law Sangu trying to drive away the water snakes rose before her eyes and when she heard the question again, she whispered: "Yes."

When he asked whether Naiwu had written the prescription himself she also murmured an affirmation.

Chen continued his searching questions: "After your husband took the medicine, did his eyes, ears, nose and mouth bleed?"

She felt as though she was being stabbed by a thousand knives. The room swayed and the posters on the wall turned upside-down. The court runners appeared to her like ghosts and demons.

"If you do not acknowledge your guilt you will be tortured," the prefect warned and he called for the finger crusher.

"Since you knew Yang Naiwu murdered your husband, why didn't you report the crime to your local *yamen*?" Chen asked.

"Because..." Xiugu stammered.

"Because he was a graduate of the provincial examination," prompted Chen, "and you an ordinary woman was not of his class?"

Xiugu mumbled: "Not of his class."

Liu Xitong breathed a sigh of relief but Chen's secretary's face darkened with anger. "This was not an interrogation at all. The prefect prompted Xiugu to confess.'' He went immediately to the inner room, brought out a teacup with a lid and ordered it to be taken to Chen Lu.

Chen lifted the lid and saw a note which read: "Interrogate Qian Baosheng of the Benevolent Pharmacy immediately."

He replaced the lid and banging his gavel ordered that Yang Naiwu be brought in.

Shouting at him he said: "You have committed adultery and murder. How dare you come to me and claim you have been wronged!"

Naiwu kowtowed and said: "I am truly wronged."

Turning to his clerk, Chen ordered him to show Naiwu Little Cabbage's confession. When he read it he cried out in despair: "I have been wronged!"

Chen's attitude totally changed: "Do you know that the law of the Qing Government stipulates that the crime of adultery is established when admitted by the woman?"

To Naiwu this was a thunderbolt from the sky.

Chen went on: "You won't confess unless torture is used."

A tiger bench was brought in and two strong court runners stripped off Naiwu's tunic and pressed his bare back on the bench. Beads of sweat broke out on his forehead while his bones crunched under the pressure of the instrument. He remained silent, then lost consciousness.

Cold water was thrown over him but still he refused to confess. "I would rather die," he said through clenched teeth. A wooden cross was brought in and he was made to kneel on the ground and his wrists were tied to each end of the cross bar while his hair was pulled tight onto the vertical bar. Two candles were lit and placed under his armpits. Black smoke rose and a stench of burning flesh spread throughout the hall.

Secretary Liu Zhaoji, unable to contain his fury, left.

To shouts of "Confess!" and the pain shooting to his heart and lungs, Naiwu eventually lost consciousness again.

Liu Xitong smiled with satisfaction.

The clerk walked up and pressed Naiwu's fingerprint on the confession which had been prepared earlier.

Back in his study, Chen's attendants helped him take off his official robe. A hot towel, a water-pipe and a cup of tea were brought to him. He looked tired after the interrogation and his nerves were strung up tight. He took a puff of his water-pipe and sipped his tea.

The Yuhang magistrate, Liu Xitong, stepped into the study and with his hands held before him said: "You must be tired, sir." Chen laughed: "You must have been scared just now during the interrogation." The expression on his face seemed to indicate that the large gifts had not been wasted.

Taking his meaning, Liu Xitong nodded vigorously.

"Fifth Concubine will play some music for you to ease your nerves," Chen said.

They walked arm-in-arm to pavilion at the back where the soft strains of a *pipa* were heard.

The table was laden with food. The two men drank while Fifth Concubine sang *Love in Four Seasons* accompanying herself on the *pipa*.

Banging the table in glee, Liu Xitong was generous

with his praises. "Wonderful! Fantastic! The music is heavenly. One doesn't find such beautiful music on earth very often."

Fifth Concubine smiled coyly and glanced at the big pearl brooch pinned on her breast and said: "I have you to thank, Mr. Liu." Chen fingered his beard and said: "When the documents arrive from the capital Yang Naiwu will be executed after the autumn harvest."

"Absolutely!" said Fifth Concubine. Hardly had she finished her words, Liu Zhaoji entered, followed by his man carrying bedding and a rattan chest. "I have come to bid you farewell," he said to his surprised superior. "I'm too old and useless now. When my advice is accepted, I stay but when it is ignored, I go."

Chen suggested he take a month's holiday but he replied: "I can't take risks. I have forebodings," he said glancing at Liu Xitong, who had gone a deep red. "When the truth of Yang Naiwu's case is known to the world one day, your future, official post and even your life..."

Chen sprang up and shouted: "Go away!"

Liu Zhaoji turned and his man followed him. As he left the *yamen* he drew a deep breath. Overhead the sky was azure blue. On the banks of the West Lake, willow trees swayed in the breeze under a bright sun.

His mind felt an easiness he had not felt before and he said to himself: "I came in without a stain on my character and I leave the same way."

The death sentence on Yang Naiwu and Little Cabbage created a wave of indignation among the officials throughout Zhejiang Province, who pleaded to the

Board of Punishments requesting a retrial. Vice minister, Xia Tongshan, who was a native of Zhejiang, intervened and the death sentence was postponed each time it was sent in. Hundreds of officials were sent to reinvestigate the case, but as they all protected each other, justice was not done. The death of the Emperor Tongzhi followed by Guangxu ascending the throne put off yet again the death sentence and, for a long time, Yang Naiwu's case was put on the shelf.

One autumn day, in the first year of the new emperor's reign, when the leaves of the Chinese parasol trees outside the heavily locked gate of the prison fluttered down in the breeze, Xiugu was sitting with the cangue around her neck when she saw a poem written on the wall by another prisoner:

"*One, two, three, four, five, high walls circle strong and tight*
Whom could the one shut in here tell her woes and wrongs?"

The poem touched her and she murmured sadly: "Master Yang, I was harmed and then I harmed you ... I was harmed and then I harmed you..." Then she screamed: "I was harmed and then I harmed you..." She wanted to die rather than carry on living. She tried to smash her head against the wall, but the wooden cangue around her neck prevented her.

Unable to kill herself made her sufferings worse and she wailed loudly. The autumn wind blew in a leaf and it slowly fell beside her. She picked it up and stared at it. Then she felt herself transported to a wooded spot where drifting golden leaves covered her. She seemed to hear Naiwu's despairing voice say: "I never thought you would do this to me, Xiugu..." She knelt down and cried: "I have betrayed you and brought misery upon you. Where are you, Master Yang?"

An autumn drizzle fell on the fallen leaves.

In the men's prison, his hair loose and in tangles, Yang Naiwu was smoothing the grey hair on his head. He recited a poem by the poet Lu You, in which he had made some changes:

Lying fettered in prison, I was not given to self pity
Still aspiring to serve the country at the borderland
Listening to the wind and rain in the tranquil night
I saw in my dream a fiery red-hot chain.

He saw before his eyes, ropes and rods, then a tiger bench and a burning wooden cross, torturing his body. He cried out in pain: "Oh heavens...."

It seemed as if Xiugu heard his cries. She rose and stumbled to the barred window but only heard the wind and the rain.

Dismal wind and sorrow-laden rain,
Demons and monsters romp wildly in the yamen.
Spring does not come to South China
Where darkness prevails everywhere.
And lovers are separated with tears and blood,
Since officials cover for each other in their wrong-doings.
The case will always remain wronged.

Xiugu gazed at the fields and cloudy sky. When could the injustice to the two lovers be pursued and the wrong righted?

Knots and Twists

IT was late autumn and the harvest had been gathered in. It was also the season for executing criminals. The execution of Yang Naiwu and Little Cabbage was postponed, only because a more important case was taking place.

It happened thus. By the West Lake the imperial travelling lodge lay sprawled along its banks.

There was an arch before the lodge and a stone tablet underneath inscribed with the words: "Civil officials must alight from their sedan chairs and military officers dismount from their horses." But one young gentleman astride a tall white horse and followed by armed servants spurred his horse on.

A guard moved forward to stop him saying that only the emperor could ride through.

An argument arose between the guard and one of the servants. "He is the son of the general," said the servant.

During the Qing Dynasty, Manchu generals were all related to the emperor, and were garrisoned in every province to supervise officials of the Han nationality.

The argument attracted a large crowd.

Guards of the imperial travelling lodge, who were all soldiers from Hunan Province, gathered round and commented: "Even a general has to dismount, so must the young master."

A Hunan soldier went to pull at the reins.

The young man raised his cudgel and hit the soldier on the head. The soldier died instantly. This annoyed his comrades who rushed up to drag the young man to court. His servants pulled out their weapons and attacked the unarmed soldiers, killing and wounding many of them as well as bystanders. The general's son went on his way in triumph as the angry soldiers and civilians carried the bodies to the *yamen* of Qiantang County, but the gate remained shut.

There was popular indignation and finally the incident reached the ears of the provincial governor, Yang Changjun. He sat grimly in his special hardwood chair, while an officer knelt before him: "They killed three of our men, Your Excellency, and wounded seven and we are unable to lodge a complaint. Your Excellency must see to it that justice is done. People are talking. They say 'The *yamen* does not listen to complaints, neither will the judicial commissioner or the provincial governor do anything to redress the wrong.'"

Yang brought his fist heavily down on the desk, abruptly rose and paced the floor.

The officer continued: "We, the troops from Hunan Province, wiped out the Taiping rebels, so that the Manchus could remain on the throne. But now…"

Yang stopped suddenly and shouted: "How dare you utter such nonsense. Leave this minute!"

As the officer rose to go, Yang said: "Give the families of the deceased and the wounded generous compensation, but the soldiers are not to create a disturbance."

Yang continued to pace the floor. Then he halted and a cunning look came into his face. He heard that the father of the young man was the garrison general and he was giving a birthday party for his favourite concubine. Yang Changjun went to offer his congratulations bringing with him an expensive gift. The general was extremely pleased and invited Yang to sit with him and his arrogant son at the main table, while his concubine filled his cup with wine. Yang sipped his wine and complimented the general: "Your son is handsome and intelligent, a brilliant son of a general. He will have a better future than you or me."

The general was pleased but had some misgivings and said: "He is a little spoiled since he is my only son now. His elder brother was killed in battle. He lounges about more than studies."

Yang laughed and reassured the general, remarking he was only sowing a few wild oats. Just then, Yang's attendant came and whispered in his ear. He rose pleading urgent business awaited him at the *yamen*. As the general saw him to the door, Yang stopped him and said: "Let your son see me to the gate." With that, he took his son's arm and together they walked out.

Outside, as the general's son was about to bow, Yang signalled to the soldiers who immediately bound and gagged the young man and galloped off with him. The governor jumped onto another horse and followed, leaving his empty sedan chair to follow slowly behind.

Gongs and drums sounded in the provincial governor's *yamen* while Yang, in an official robe, together with the treasurer and judge, bowed to a sword conferred on him by the emperor which gave him the authority to kill. To the sound of gongs and drums they knelt three times and kowtowed nine times to the sword.

The general's son was tied to a pillar, and swore as he raged: "Our family have served the imperial court for three generations. How dare you do this to me?"

Holding up the sword Yang asked him if he recognized it.

Cold sweat stood out on the young man's forehead as he saw the imperial sword which had the power to execute him without seeking the permission of the emperor.

Yang said: "You rode roughshod into the imperial travelling lodge, killed Hunan soldiers who have done outstanding deeds in battle, taking advantage of your background, but the people have many grievances against you."

He ordered the military officer: "Cut off his head."

The provincial judge gave a thumbs-up sign in admiration: "The execution of this evil-doer will raise the morale of the Hunan soldiers," he said. "Well done!"

A report was sent to the imperial court notifying them of the execution, and also about the lack of discipline displayed by the general towards his son, which allowed him to behave wantonly, upsetting the people. The Empress Dowager Cixi had no alternative but to dismiss the general from his post and transfer him back to Beijing.

Ladies-in-waiting stood outside the majestic Lamasery of Harmony and Peace in Beijing as the Empress Dowager emerged after worshipping to return to the palace.

The disgraced general who had been waiting outside, moved forward and kowtowed to her. "Old Buddha, I deserve to be put to death," he said.

The Empress Dowager sighed: "Your son's

behaviour in Hangzhou was shocking. If I did not dismiss you, the people there would have been too angry. I have to agree with Yang Changjun's report."

The old general pleaded for mercy and she gave him the post of military governor of Rehe Province. As he bowed in gratitude she called out: "Wait! Tell me more about the case of Yang Naiwu and Little Cabbage. Were they wronged?" The general, although burning with hatred as he thought of how Yang Changjun had killed his son, controlled his feelings and gave a perfunctory answer. "Although the officials have gone through the case they seem justified in their findings, but the people of Zhejiang think differently. I have no idea of the truth."

The Empress Dowager ordered her eunuch to write out a directive to the provincial authorities of Zhejiang to re-examine the case.

Xiugu had languished in prison for three years and had no more tears to shed. She was going to pay with her life in exchange for her young sister-in-law and for the peace of the Ge household. But her heart bled as she thought of how she had caused the bankruptcy of Yang Naiwu's family.

Naiwu's sister, Shuying, bribed the wardress at the women's prison with three silver dollars and together with the family's faithful servant, Chen Laode, asked to see Xiugu, who upon seeing them tried to retreat, fearing they were there to seek revenge on her. Shuying took her arm instead and helped her to a chair. Xiugu lowered her head with shame as she saw the accusing eyes of Chen Laode.

Shuying said kindly: "You're much thinner."

Chen Laode added: "It seems to me she enjoys

good health. Only her conscience is bad. Because of her, Mr. Yang is no longer a *juren*, because of her, the family had to sell its property, and because of her my master's life is at stake. I would like to cut her heart out and see if it is red or black."

Shuying stopped him and offered Xiugu some pastries: "I have something to confide in you." The offering of food made Xiugu feel more at ease but she was astonished when Shuying asked for forgiveness. "It was I who told your mother-in-law to get you married off to Xiaoda. I separated you and Naiwu by sending him to study in Suzhou and as a result have created misery for you both."

Xiugu knelt down before her and said in tears: "It was I who have brought misfortune to Master Yang."

Now that the mutual suspicion had been dispelled, Shuying asked for the truth regarding the death of Xiugu's husband. She said nothing but sobbed bitterly.

Chen Laode could not keep silent and said: "Don't ask her, young mistress. When the document arrives from the capital she will be cut thirty-six times. I will then kill myself and wait in hell to skin her."

Xiugu burst out: "You are justified in cursing me. I repaid Master Yang's kindness by harming him. I am a vicious woman. I was cheated by them. It was all their doing... They have destroyed me and then I destroyed him. Tell your brother that we are finished in this life. In the next one I will repay him by being his dog or horse."

Shuying seized her: "You mean you still want to save my brother?"

She answered that she was willing to die a thousand deaths to save him.

Shuying told her that the Empress Dowager had ordered the provincial officials to re-open the case and hoped that Xiugu would expose the real murderer.

Xiugu heaved a long sigh and agreed.

Chen Laode promised: "When you have saved my master, you will be executed of course but I'll put on mourning clothes for you."

She answered: "I don't deserve such kindness," and promised that she would reveal the identity of the murderer in court. Shuying and Chen Laode knelt down to Xiugu who, unable to stop them, did the same.

It was night and there was a full moon. Provincial Judge Kuai, accompanied by Chen Lu, the prefect of Hangzhou, stepped out of the door of the back garden of the *yamen* and stood beside the green waters of the West Lake. The lake was at its best in the moonlight. Strains of music drifted out from a gaily-painted pleasure boat which lay anchored at the bank.

The two men moved over to the boat, waiting and wondering why the provincial governor had not arrived. A servant then informed them that he was reading up the Yang Naiwu case and was unable to take part in the outing on the lake. As it moved slowly away from the bank, the two men were being lavishly entertained by beautifully dressed ladies with heavy makeup. The men laughed as two girls played the one instrument. Another girl plucked a *pipa* while another pressed the strings. A fifth girl began to sing.

The boat moved leisurely towards the centre of the lake famous for a scenic spot called "Three Pools Reflecting the Moon''. Three hollow stone pagodas built during the Ming Dynasty stood lit up by candles placed inside which shone through the thin paper pasted over circles cut out of the stone, making fifteen large and small round spots reflected in the water. Together with the reflection of the three moons in the three pools the place was like a magical fairyland as the boat sailed by. Lanterns mixed with the moonlight and candles, the reflections of the moon, the pagodas and the clouds merged together which called to mind a line of poetry which began:

> "*Autumn is melted in the shimmering waters of the lake.*"

The prefect and Judge Kuai stood at the prow. The judge had been a military man but had not touched a bow and arrow nor rode on horseback for many years. In an extremely good mood he drew a bow and aimed at one of the holes in the pagoda. Twang, the arrow flew straight in, extinguishing the candle. All the ladies on the boat sang his praises.

Prefect Chen said obsequiously: "Your Excellency is as indomitable as in the past."

The judge was flattered. "I'm getting on in years," he replied.

Chen waved away the women and the servants and the two men were alone.

The judge asked why he had been invited to the boat and Chen answered that he thought he needed some relaxation after so many criminal cases he had tried.

The judge glanced contentedly at his former subordinate and, patting his protruding stomach, said: "Our present successes are due to our feats in the numerous battles we fought against the Taipings."

Chen answered: "But some people are jealous and want to squeeze us out. More than a hundred officials have gone through Yang Naiwu's case but the vice-minister of the Board of Punishments, Xia Tongshan, is creating trouble for us, rejecting the sentences every time they are sent in. These officials are all former Hunan troops who went through a lot with our commanders."

The old judge was incensed: "Under no circumstances will we allow these Zhejiang people squeeze us out. Our bodies are covered with wounds and scars. It is we who have protected this country."

Chen pressed home his point: "Exactly. It is we and the Hunan troops who wiped out the Taipings and recovered Hangzhou. The Zhejiang officials are now trying to make use of the Yang Naiwu case to destroy us. You must give us your support, Your Excellency."

A man in military uniform came out from the cabin, strode over to Judge Kuai and knelt down on one knee. It was Liu Zihe, Little Cabbage's seducer in disguise.

"Don't you recognize me, Your Excellency," he asked. "You must remember our attack at the Taipings' capital. We fought tenaciously against the Long Hairs and stormed the palace of the Heavenly King."

Judge Kuai was transported as he remembered the battle scene.

Liu Zihe went on in an impassioned voice: "You

were wounded in the arm, and the blood dripped onto your saddle and you fell. I dressed your wound and then went back into battle and we stormed into the palace. Our soldiers broke out into *The Song of Victory.*"

He began singing it again and the judge and prefect joined in. The bold and unrestrained singing rose and fell above the lake, and when they finished they broke into loud laughter.

Kuai looked with pleasure at Liu Zihe dressed in his officer's uniform. "I have often related that incident to Prefect Chen and have been wanting to meet you again for a long time to reward you."

Liu Zihe quickly went down on his knees. "As the saying goes: 'When all the birds are killed, the bow and arrows are put away.' I'm afraid I am soon to lose my life."

Chen interrupted: "His father is the present magistrate of Yuhang, the first interrogator of Yang Naiwu. If the Zhejiang officials have their way, his father will not only have no future but might be executed and his property confiscated."

Liu, full of indignation, said: "When storming the palace of the Heavenly King, I never thought that a brave solder such as I would one day be a victim of slander and jealousy."

Chen added: "One takes into account the owner of the dog when intending to beat it. But the Zhejiang officials do not care. They are jealous of our success and ability and are making use of this case to trap us."

Liu remained kneeling. "I would rather die here before Your Excellency. I don't want my father and me to suffer insults at the hands of the Zhejiang officials." He rose and pulled out his sword as though intending to fall on it.

Judge Kuai shouted: "Halt!"

Liu froze.

"The Hunan troops are not all dead," he said. "The provincial governor will look into the matter."

Prefect Chen whispered into Kuai's ear: "His father is on good terms with Mr. Bao the Grand Councillor."

"Under such circumstances, maybe Yang Naiwu is not wrong..." Kuai knitted his brows in thought. "Or is he...?"

Chen answered: "Yang Naiwu is extremely cunning. Don't you remember two years ago...?"

Kuai recalled an incident two years earlier when a favourite horse of his was suddenly engulfed in a freak wave beside the Qiantang River and carried away and drowned. He had the groom stripped to the waist and flogged saying his life was nothing compared to that of his horse. He was flogged until he lost consciousness. The groom's wife appealed to Naiwu to save his life. Shocked he had written:

"When his stable caught fire, Confucius was more concerned about human beings than horses. When waves rolled in at Qiantang River, the provincial judge was more concerned about his horse than humans."

Judge Kuai had been peacefully smoking his waterpipe when his secretary read out what had been written and slammed down his pipe as the meaning was explained.

Kuai was unable to punish Yang Naiwu, as the Qing Government held Confucius in high esteem and Yang Naiwu was a well-known scholar and reluctantly set the groom free.

As the three men sailed around the serene lake, Kuai's emotions were in a tumult. "Yang Naiwu is really a cunning man," he commented.

How could such a pettifogger claim he had been wronged. Yet the Zhejiang officials are making use of his case now....

"Bah!" the judge said. "They are daydreaming!"

Officials Cover Up for Officials

THE *yamen* belonging to the governor of Zhejiang Province was an imposing building with its upturned eaves. The governor, Yang Changjun, a tall stout man in his fifties, with big eyes, thick brows and stubbly beard, was reading Yang Naiwu's case when a servant announced the arrival of the Provincial Treasurer Fan and Provincial Judge Kuai.

The two visitors straightened their sleeves, hastened in and asked after his health.

Wasting no time, Yang said: "I have read the entire case and I do not believe the accused is guilty of killing the husband to get the wife. It is more likely they first committed adultery and then killed the husband."

"Your Excellency is absolutely right," said the treasurer, a thin old man well-versed in matters of official bureaucracy and as slippery as an eel, able to take equivocal attitudes.

Yang continued: "This case has been investigated by over a hundred officials and each time their reports have been overturned by the Board of Punishments. Today, the three of us are going to get to the bottom of this matter to show that Zhejiang Province is not without men of principle."

It was an exceptional occasion for three important representatives of Zhejiang Province to discuss the case.

The courtroom was solemn and silent with court runners and clerks standing on either side.

The prefects of the four counties — fourth-grade officials — who had handled Yang Naiwu's case filed in, evidently in fear and trepidation.

Next came the magistrates — seventy grade officials. They were on tenterhooks too.

Soon the desks of the three presiding officials were piled high with the documents from the lower officials, who lined up on both sides according to rank.

Chen Lu and Liu Xitong stole glances at the three men in top authority.

The governor looked extremely grim. The treasurer was expressionless and the judge's demeanour cold and forbidding.

Xiugu was brought in wearing the cangue and in chains.

Yang said sternly: "This case has dragged on for years. You first confessed that Yang Naiwu murdered your husband to get you, then you changed your story and said you both murdered your husband after committing adultery. Which is the truth?"

He warned her of dire punishment if she said anything but the truth and pointed to the whips, rods, rattan canes and finger crusher as well as other torture instruments.

Xiugu only saw the picture of Shuying pleading to her to save her brother's life and Naiwu crying out that he had been wronged, and ignoring the torture instruments she cried out: "Yang Naiwu has been wronged! My seducer was another man!"

The new development was a total surprise for the three men. The officials standing around went pale, some wiping cold sweat from their brows, others touching their colleagues in apprehension.

Liu Zihe's blood ran cold, as he heard Xiugu's words.

Chen Laode was overjoyed and ran out of the courtyard to where his master, Naiwu, was imprisoned in a wooden cage outside the gate. He shouted: "You're saved, master. Xiugu has admitted to the real seducer."

Tears streamed down as Naiwu knelt down and cried: "Heaven has eyes!"

Judge Kuai banged his gavel on the desk and shouted: "Xiugu, how dare you tell lies in the governor's courtroom?"

She answered fearlessly: "Just now, Your Excellency said I would be tortured if I told lies. That is why I am now telling the truth. Yet you still order punishment. This is too..." she lowered her head, feeling wronged.

The treasurer asked: "Who was your seducer, then?" Liu Xitong and his son Zihe shook with fear.

Xiugu spoke clearly: "My seducer is Qian Baosheng, the young proprietor of the Benevolent Pharmacy."

Chen Laode ran back to Naiwu: "She has admitted the man was Qian Baosheng." Naiwu looked very dubious.

Since he had been called only as a witness, Qian Baosheng walked into the courtroom with a confident air.

But his confidence soon evaporated when the magistrate accused him of being Xiugu's lover.

Qian stammered: "She's lying. Just look at my face. Can I be a match for her?"

He was, to be true, no oil-painting. His nose had disintegrated due to venereal disease. Little Cabbage was far too beautiful in contrast.

All eyes turned to the judge and he realized that he was expected to take over the questioning.

He snapped: "Have the torture instruments prepared."

When they were thrown towards Qian, he cried out in fright: "Your Excellency, to catch a thief, you seize the booty, to catch the adulterers, you seize the pair. To hang a man's life on the words of a woman. That's too flimsy. Let me confront Xiugu."

Xiugu had appeared in public so often that she was no longer the shy little girl of yore and especially now when she was determined to save Naiwu's life. She said: "Hello, Baosheng, you're here too."

It made him jump in fright to see such a calm woman who had always blushed scarlet before strange men in the past.

Experience had taught Xiugu that officials covered up for each other so it would be much better to make Qian Baosheng to tell the truth.

She said defiantly: "One day in mid-July, in the twelfth year of the reign of Emperor Tongzhi, on the pretext of asking me to do some embroidery work, you drugged and raped me and since I was stained, I let you have your way ever since. When my husband returned home, you hated to see me belong to him, so when he fell ill you fed him arsenic."

"Did you hate me?" asked Qian.

"I would have liked to skin you alive," she replied.

"Then you should have reported me to the *yamen* at that time."

Xiugu was lost for words but eventually said: "Because you begged me not to..."

The court was so tense and quiet hardly a breath stirred the air.

The judge banged his gavel: "What more do you have to say, you scoundrel?" he asked.

Qian gulped but said nothing, while Liu Zihe and his father shook with fear again.

Judge Kuai was quite sure that Qian was so ugly he could not possibly be Little Cabbage's real seducer. But if he should own up under torture to the true identity then Yang Naiwu would have to be declared innocent and over a hundred officials would have to be dismissed. The Hunanese would really be squeezed out by the Zhejiang officials.

The judge ordered an adjournment.

In the study the three presiding officials discussed the unexpected turn of events and what tactics to adopt now. Judge Kuai reiterated that the real reason for the Zhejiang officials' desire to overturn the verdict was to seek the dismissal of the hundred or so officials involved: "They are people who have fought so many battles for you, it is just a cunning manoeuvre."

The treasurer asked: "You mean they are beating the dog as well as its master?"

Governor Yang brought his fist down on the table and stood up. "They haven't got a hope! I'll see who can reverse this case with iron-clad evidence!"

The three officials entered the courtroom again.

The judge fixed his gaze on Qian Baosheng: "Little Cabbage has already owned up. Are you going to confess?"

Qian answered: "I would like to know how long our affair was supposed to have lasted."

Xiugu replied: "Two months."

"Then," said Qian, "she will be able to tell the court where I have a particular scar on my body. If she can't then she cannot accuse me of adultery."

Qian's reasoning fitted in with the judge's wishes. He turned an enquiring eye towards Xiugu.

She answered: "We were not husband and wife, he came to me at night."

"One could tell where my scar is even in hell," said Qian.

Xiugu was trapped: "On his foot," she said.

Qian smiled in relief. He asked for paper and pen and drew a picture before folding it up and handing it to the judge.

The judge was disgusted by what he saw and he could have had Qian flogged but instead he ordered that he be examined.

The examination confirmed Qian's drawing. It was shown to Xiugu whose face turned scarlet and a finger crusher was prepared.

Desperation made her try one more attempt. "I'll tell the truth," she cried. "My love for Yang Naiwu deepened when he became a *juren*. So I killed my husband in order to marry him. When he found out the truth, he spurned me, so my love turned to hatred and I pinned the murder on him."

Liu Zihe and his father heaved a sigh of relief.

The judge thought: "Xiugu has taken the blame. The Board of Punishments is not likely to refute this and the case will be closed. Yang Naiwu will be free and the officials will be heavily reprimanded…"

He looked at the official hats and cried: "What a brazen hussy. You're still in love with Yang Naiwu and are trying to extricate him. Bring on the lighted brazier!"

Her tunic was torn off and a court runner picked out a red hot piece of wire with a pair of pliers and placed it on her tender body.

In chains, Yang Naiwu was pushed into the courtroom. Kneeling down, he prostrated himself and cried: "Flog me!" This was a very odd request and everyone was baffled. No prisoner had ever asked for a flogging.

Governor Yang banged his gavel and said: "You are too defiant. There has never been a flogging before an interrogation."

"In that case," said Naiwu, "you are all upright officials? I have gone through dozens of interrogations and beaten in each one. I'm covered with wounds and scars."

He was taken away and examined and it bore out his words. The report said: "He has been burnt with a chain once, burnt in the armpits three times, his legs crushed by rods five times and scars caused by whippings cover his back."

The three top officials were astonished. They were unaware that torture had been administered like this. Liu Xitong and Chen Lu looked at each other in constemation.

The judge jeered: "But Xiugu has admitted you had an affair with her and murdered her husband. What can you say?"

Naiwu gave a cold smile. He pointed to the dazzling

semi-precious beads of office on the hats of the officials. Red beads for first and second-grade officials, blue for the fourth and fifth grades and white for sixth and seventh grades. The governor was a full second grade, the treasurer a second grade and the judge third grade. A prefect was fourth grade and a magistrate was seventh grade. Pointing to the beads, he said: "These beads are worth a lot of money. Some are priceless. I have only a useless head. The future of an official is invaluable while people's lives are worthless. I hope that you'll safeguard your beads of office instead of creating bad feelings with your colleagues. Let me be wronged to the end."

A prisoner offering advice to his interrogator in front of such a large gathering was unheard of.

Controlling his fury with difficulty, the judge said: "I'm impartial and incorruptible. I'll handle this case fairly. Although you're extremely learned, you are actually a lecherous man. Have the torture instruments made ready."

Naiwu was stripped of his clothes. A hollow tin tube shaped like a snake was wrapped round his body. A brazier with a cauldron of boiling oil was brought in.

Although the Qing Government forbade torture, this particular *yamen* had no scruples about using this method of pouring boiling oil into the mouth of the "snake" where it ran through the hollow tube thereby causing burns as it twisted round the victim's body. Death would have been preferable than the pain which would leave one crippled. Xiugu was brought in to witness the torture.

She saw the tin snake twisting round Naiwu's body. A court runner ladled out the oil, raising it high in order to pour it into the mouth of the "snake".

She screamed out: "Master Yang..." and as the people turned to stare at her, she mumbled: "Admit your guilt." Yang Naiwu had not expected her to pin the murder onto him in the presence of such high authority and he glared at her with hatred in his eyes as he said: "You can get anything with torture." He picked up a brush and signed the confession and then tossed the brush away.

As Xiugu looked around her she seemed to see the poster "Honesty and Uprightness" topple down on Naiwu, crushing him beneath it. The demons and monsters she had seen the other night in her nightmare swooped over her as she made to go towards the unconscious Naiwu but she was pulled back by the prison guards and taken away.

A Long Dark Night

ONCE again, under cruel torture, Yang Naiwu was forced to confess that he and Little Cabbage had committed adultery and conspired to murder her husband. He was thrown into a condemned cell to await execution after the autumn harvest. Little Cabbage would be slashed many times with a knife and then beheaded.

The people of Hangzhou knew this was an unjust verdict and many officials and scholars protested. The trial was eventually reported in the Shanghai newspaper *Shenbao* and the news spread throughout the country.

Yao Shifa, an elderly uncle of Yang Naiwu, was a *yamen* courier and he was returning to Hangzhou from Sichuan Province in far-away west China. As he trudged along the precipitous mountain paths, he rested by a pavilion to drink some water from a stream and sat down to smoke his pipe. He got into conversation with a merchant who, learning that the old courier was a native of Zhejiang, told him about the case which had set the country by the ears. He produced some copies of the Shanghai newspaper. When Naiwu's uncle read the name of his nephew he was very perturbed. He bade a hasty farewell to the merchant and travelled posthaste to Hangzhou.

Naiwu's house had been sold to cover the cost of

the lawsuits. Shuying, her son and Naiwu's bride Cuifeng had moved to a one-storey house with bare walls. When Yao finally found them Shuying was ill and Cuifeng was giving her medicine.

His eyes filled with tears as they related the past sad happenings. "Don't take things too much to heart," he said comfortingly. "Being a courier all these years has taught me something. To live in this world, one must be very careful so that nothing will happen to one. And when something does happen, you mustn't be afraid. Now you must tell me everything in the minutest detail."

Shuying recounted all the steps she had taken to seek justice for Naiwu, even appealing to the Empress Dowager who had ordered the Zhejiang authorities to re-examine the case. But the same bribery and corruption had taken place and there seemed to be no hope.

Yao questioned them closely and learned that Little Cabbage had, during one of her interrogations, referred to a different man. "Then," said Yao, "it must be someone with influence. He is no ordinary person. That's who she was afraid to tell. As I am familiar with all the *yamens* in Beijing __ the capital __ I might be able to find someone willing to help and seek an official with a red bead on his cap to be sent here to unearth the truth."

Shuying got up from her sick bed with difficulty and knelt down to pray before the memorial tablets of her dead parents.

Cuifeng bent one knee before Yao.

"Don't thank me yet," he said. "There are so many wronged cases in this country, it might be useless, but my old bones are used to hardships."

In the women's prison, there was a clang of the iron door, and a harsh voice ordered Xiugu out.

She cringed in the corner but a goaler stepped in and dragged her out. He said: "You're not going to the execution ground. Don't be afraid."

They passed through a long corridor, and she was pushed into a jail officer's room, where she saw a pot of wine and a bowl of meat on the table.

She turned to escape but the door banged shut and she was unable to get out.

A pair of rough hands touched her as the figure of a prison officer loomed before her.

"Be a good girl," he said. "You've been untouched for two whole years. So fresh and beautiful! Give me a taste of you...."

He tore off a piece of her clothing and then beckoned to a wardress: "Give her a good wash." Xiugu's screams were smothered as a basin of cold water was poured over her and she collapsed on the ground. The wardress stooped down and wiped her body roughly as Xiugu covered her face with her hands and struggled. The officer said: "Don't be shy. Everyone loves Little Cabbage, particularly when washed...."

She fought and bit the hands of the wardress as they tore away the rest of her clothing. The officer said: "You let Yang Naiwu do it. Why shouldn't I do it too?"

Xiugu tore away from their grasp and tried to dash her head against the wall. The wardress took fright and threw the torn tunic over the hysterical girl's head. "Let's call it off," she said. "If she hurts herself, we'll be in trouble."

As Xiugu was dragged back to her cell, she trod on a sharp pointed stone. The pain brought her back to her senses and she heard the night watchman calling miserably: "All is well."

The night was long and the sky was dark. Whom could Little Cabbage turn to for help and where was she being taken?...

Singing and Tears

MOST influential officials and aristocrats in Hangzhou lived in Guanqian Street where their mansions all had vermillion gates with imposing stone lions of all sizes and postures at the entrance. Right behind the gate was a screen wall blocking the view into the courtyard.

A listless Xiugu was taken to the inner quarters of the *yamen*. Prefect Chen and his wife were entertaining guests around a table laden with sumptuous food, most of which was untouched.

The guests, after three rounds of wine, were a little tipsy, and no one had yet tasted the steamed fish with vinegar and the meat cooked in the Tang-dynasty's Hangzhou governor Su Dongpo's favourite way.

Prefect Chen's wife turned to the provincial treasurer: "You're the guest of honour today. If you do not sample the fish first, no one will."

The wife of the provincial treasurer said: "I think everyone is waiting for Little Cabbage to boost their spirits." Her husband answered: "Nonsense. I saw enough of her when I interrogated her. It was you who insisted on seeing her."

His wife replied: "Well, you said you were too busy tonight, so why did you finally come with me?"

Another woman guest pointed to the man sitting beside her: "He played the same trick."

Everyone broke out laughing.

Forgetting her usual air of one who had been conferred a title by the emperor, she retorted: "People say that Xiugu has such a beautiful willowy figure that Yang Naiwu sacrificed a promising career for love of her. So if you men can feast your eyes on her, why shouldn't we?"

The provincial treasurer's wife said: "Let me lay down a rule now. When Little Cabbage is brought in, all the men, regardless of rank, must leave the room. Agreed?"

Prefect Chen and his wife exchanged glances. "Ladies," said Chen, "the imperial court has not given its opinion on this case yet. Today, my wife and I have invited you here specifically to see for yourself the viciousness of a woman with such good looks and also for the officials present to observe Little Cabbage's actions, expression and what she says, to find some clues."

The provincial treasurer piped up: "That's right. You are killing two birds with one stone."

"It was very thoughtful of Prefect Chen and his wife," said one of the guests. "But what a pity the provincial judge, the governor and his wife are not here."

Mrs. Chen glanced at the wife of the provincial judge: "They did not want to come. The governor's wife told me that her husband was in a bad mood. Because he had the son of a general killed the father has now gone to the capital to complain to the emperor."

Prefect Chen then asked the judge's wife why her husband hadn't come. She answered: "When he heard the governor was in a bad mood he became depressed too."

The treasurer said: "The two of them carry considerable weight. They're not like me. As long as the money in the treasury is safe, I can enjoy a little debauchery without criticism."

His wife butted in: "Except you have to get my permission first."

There was more laughter.

Liu Xitong, sitting in the most insignificant seat, ventured: "Gentlemen, I hear that some of the Zhejiang officials in the province are sending secret reports to the imperial court about Yang Naiwu and Little Cabbage. They are creating difficulties for all those officials of Hunan origin who handled the case. That is why the Board of Punishments has taken a long time to return the documents. If the case is overturned, things will be very bad."

"They wouldn't dare," the judge's wife said with a sour expression.

Another official reminded Liu Xitong of his good relationship with the Grand Counciller Bao.

Liu agreed: "He once thought well enough of me to recommend me to the post of prefect of Yinxian…"

The judge's wife smacked her lips in appreciation: "Well, well, the saying goes that 'Shaoxing is a place for copper, Jiaxing a place for silver, Ningbo a place for gold,' and to be a prefect of Yinxian one could amass a hundred thousand taels of silver in ten years. Why didn't you accept the post?"

Liu sighed: "It's a long story why I was obliged to choose such an unfortunate place as Yuhang."

The prefect's wife tugged at the judge's wife's sleeve: "Look. They've brought Little Cabbage."

A maid pushed Xiugu in and ordered her to kneel before the officials and their ladies and pulled her face up towards the assembled guests.

There were murmurs of admiration when they saw her beautiful face.

The prefect's wife said: "You mustn't be afraid. These titled ladies and myself are all aware you spent three years in chains in prison. Although there is proof of your guilt, we pity the misery you have gone through for one so young. That's why we invited the officials here tonight. If you have anything that you were unwilling to say in court, tell us now."

Xiugu shook her head.

Liu Xitong said: "It was all Yang Naiwu's fault. He got close to you by not charging you rent and then taught you to read. The prefect and I will plead to the judge for leniency if you will tell us how he enticed you...."

Her torturer's hypocrisy filled Xiugu with rage and her eyes flashed with anger.

The judge's wife urged her: "Pour everything out and don't hold anything back ... not one single bit...."

One of the officials, whose eyes had been rivetted on Little Cabbage, said: "You must make good use of the chance tonight. Put us in a good mood while we are drinking, and we can change the death sentence to imprisonment. Then after a few years you can be released. We have the power to do that."

Xiugu had learnt a hard lesson during the last three years and did not trust officials at all, especially the group staring at her with lascivious eyes while the wives looked at her as if she were a dog or cat.

The treasurer's wife said coldly: "The saying is

true: 'When a woman with slanting shoulders commits adultery, she leaves no trace. A waist tiny as a snake attracts bees and butterflies'."

The judge's wife added: "A woman with long legs and small feet seduces many men."

Xiugu thought to herself: "People like you can talk like saints but in reality you are all criminals and worthless women."

A maid whispered to the prefect and his wife: "Little Cabbage sings ballads well."

The judge, now quite tipsy, cried out: "Excellent. Get her to sing and dance at the same time!"

Xiugu saw the maid peeling a pear, which reminded her of happier times when she was in Naiwu's study. She had sung and peeled fruit for him. Without realizing, she began to sing:

> "*I hold the tiny knife in my hand,*
> *Peeling sugarcane and then water chestnuts.*
> *Yes, I peel the water chestnuts, the sugar cane*
> *And hand it to my love and in his mouth,*
> *Sweeter than honey, Oh yes, sweeter than honey.*
>
> *You ask me why your sweetheart*
> *Would not peel the pear.*
> *Pear symbolizes separation*
> *You and I must not eat the pear,*
> *We do not want to part,*
> *Oh no, we do not want to part.*"

Only when Xiugu saw the pleased and satisfied expressions of the audience, did she realize she had subconsciously transported herself back to the time when she had known happiness.

The old courier, Yao Shifa, had spent two months of hard travelling before arriving in the capital. When he came to the Board of Civil Service, in his dust-covered clothes, he was stopped by the guard who shouted: "Hey, what are you doing here?"

He bowed deeply: "I have come to see the military secretary, Mr. Wang."

The guard, seeing Yao's travel-stained clothes, was reluctant to announce him. Yao pleaded that he held a government post and if he consented to let him through, he would invite him to wine and food in the evening. But when the military secretary had heard Yao out, he shook his head.

He was familiar with the case and was aware that even the vice-minister of the Board of Punishments was unable to have the case redressed. The Board of Civil Service could do even less. In the end he suggested that Yao should try the Court of Censors. But he doubted that it would be of any use. In the autumn Yang Naiwu and Little Cabbage would be executed.

An Unexpected Breakthrough

WITH his trips to the Board of Civil Service and the Court of Censors a failure, Yao headed for the *yamen* of the commander-in-chief in charge of security in the capital. The gate was guarded by armed men. Smiling, Yao handed his written complaint to an officer who, after glancing at it, threw it on the ground. When Yao bent to pick it up the officer kicked him hard and snapped: "What a nerve to bring such a trivial case of debauchery to the *yamen* of the commander-in-chief!"

Yao pleaded on his knees: "Please forgive me, my lord. This is the last place I could come to. Please look over this case. The defendants have been atrociously wronged. You'll be saving lives."

The officer ordered his men to throw him out and poor Yao Shifa, in his seventies, had to retreat under whacking canes.

At the Palace of Peaceful Longevity situated in the Forbidden City in the centre of the capital where yellow-glazed tiled roofs sent out a golden glow under the sun, a performance of Peking opera was being played before the Empress Dowager Cixi, accompanied by her ladies-in-waiting, in the Pavilion of Delightful Music. Titled ministers sat in the winding corridors on the ground floor while Cixi on the first floor. The last item of the performance was *The Fourth Son of the Yangs Visits*

His Mother. The excellent coloratura of the opera singer pleased the Empress Dowager and she smiled.

The chief eunuch, Li Lianying, moved forward a step and in an oily voice said softly to her: "No matter how well the actor plays the part of the Empress Dowager Xiao, she is not a patch on the way you carry yourself."

This made Cixi very happy and she ordered large rewards for the performers. "My fortieth birthday is approaching and I'm in good spirits. You may announce that the ministers sitting in the corridors can come and sit by me if they wish to do so."

The chief eunuch said: "The Old Buddha's good mood is a sign that the Qing Dynasty will last for many generations." He bowed and went downstairs.

The ministers were overwhelmed by this unexpected favour but none dared to make a move.

One of the supervising censors, Tian Shurui, rose, took a few steps, halted and pulled out a memorial to the throne and carefully read it once again.

Another censor and a clerk of the inner court walked up and asked him if he wished to hand in the memorial to the Empress Dowager but the clerk suggested giving it in the next day at court, so that she could continue enjoying the performance.

Tian replied: "I want to speak to her in person while she is in a good mood. It is a matter of life and death concerning a new provincial graduate. It is urgent." He gave the memorial to the censor.

The censor read it and said: "The Empress Dowager has already ordered the Provincial Governor Yang to investigate the case in person. I should think twice before bringing this case up again before Her Majesty."

Tian raised his eyes and looked up at the Empress Dowager chatting happily with her chief eunuch and ladies-in-waiting. He took the memorial back, lifted the front of his long gown and ascended the stairs.

Gazing after him the clerk snorted: "He doesn't want his official hat anymore."

Tian went down on his knees and kowtowed. "Please accept my greetings to the Empress Dowager," he said. As it was a supervising censor, the Empress Dowager said: "Today the sovereign and her subordinates are enjoying themselves. Can't you wait until tomorrow?"

Tian answered: "Because of Your Majesty's good fortune, we have had no trouble from the natives in the north or from the foreigners in the south, but some of your officials in the provinces do not follow your instructions, believing you are only the regent for the young emperor and so you are not given information dealing with matters farther away."

The suggestion that some provincial officials might be disobeying her orders annoyed the Empress Dowager, who pulled a long face and said: "Is that so? Tell me about it."

Tian, encouraged, went on: "I heard that the provincial governor of Zhejiang, Yang Changjun, is becoming more and more covetous and grasping. He gets confessions extracted by torture and his verdicts are flippant and arbitrary. He regards human life less than a straw. When your Imperial Majesty ordered him to look personally into the case, he allowed the provincial judge and treasurer to handle it. He is deceiving the imperial court and misleading the people."

The Empress Dowager asked: "Are you referring to the Yang Naiwu and Little Cabbage case?"

"Exactly," answered Tian. "This may be a trivial case of ordinary people but it is a most complicated and intriguing case. Many articles have been published in the Shanghai newspaper claiming an injustice has been perpetrated. If this case drags on the prestige of the imperial court will suffer. I humbly urge that the Old Buddha choose another capable official to re-examine the case. This will prove you take public opinion into account and treasure human life."

Just then, Li Lianying, the eunuch, announced: "Old Buddha, your newly appointed literary chancellor of Zhejiang, Hu Ruilan, has come to bid you farewell before he leaves for his post."

The chancellor kowtowed and asked if there were any orders.

"Tian Shurui has submitted a memorial here," said the Empress Dowager.

"Go and find out the truth about the case the first thing when you get to Hangzhou. I'll give you my written order at the court tomorrow morning."

Tian then said to Hu: "I hope you will make a thorough investigation of the case and be worthy of the responsibility given to you by the Empress Dowager." He added, "The contortions in this case are as woven as a cocoon and it requires someone like you, with no personal interests, to unravel it. Otherwise one will never get to the bottom of it."

The eunuch, speaking before the Empress Dowager, said: "The Old Buddha enjoys happiness and a long life. All wrongs in the country will certainly be righted. Your Majesty's birthday is approaching and the whole country will celebrate with her."

Beaming with pleasure the Empress Dowager told Hu: "Yang Naiwu is a poor new provincial graduate. If you can find him innocent, do not hesitate to do so."

Early the following morning, the old courier, Yao Shifa, limped out from the inn. He sighed at the hazy sun, walked down the street and stopped at a stall for some corn buns and a sup of wine before leaving for Yuhang.

At the same time, Military Secretary Wang of the Board of Civil Service, a clerk from the Court of Censors, and a military officer were going from inn to inn looking for him.

They eventually found him at the stall and Wang grabbed him saying: "Come and lodge your complaint, old fellow." Yao shook his head: "I'm not lodging complaints any more."

Wang patted him on the shoulder: "We have been ordered to find you by the newly appointed literary councillor after hearing you had come to the capital to lodge the complaint."

Yao gave a wry smile: "Newly appointed or not, they are all the same pot of fish. It's useless."

Wang replied: "You're a queer fish. Three days ago, when I tried to talk you out of your petition, you insisted on carrying on with it. Now you are dropping it. Why?"

Yao replied: "They nearly broke three of my ribs." He lifted his clothes and revealed a large plaster on his chest.

"I'm going home out of harm's way." He took

152 The Scholar and the Serving Maid

to his heels but the military officer lifted him onto his horse: "I have my orders to take you to the councillor."

The situation was such:

*A big stage as the world is
One's future is hard to tell.
At the end of one's tether
There's no way out.
Can one expect to live
In such circumstances?*

Shedding Blood in the Yamen

NEWS spread quickly in the streets and lanes of Hangzhou that the new literary chancellor of the city, Hu Ruilan, had been sent as an imperial commissioner with the mission to re-examine the case of Yang Naiwu and Little Cabbage. When he arrived he refused to see any of the local civilian and military officials. When three weeks passed with not a single move from him, people began to talk.

One said: "The literary chancellor is a *jinshi*, a palace graduate of the highest imperial exams. He is not like those who have bought their official titles and posts and accept bribes to bend the law."

Another retorted: "It's hard to say what he has up his sleeve."

Hu was carefully studying the documents relating to the case and found something which made him slap the desk in glee and cry out loud. Just then the military secretary came in to announce softly: "Mr. Yang, the provincial governor, has called. He is not wearing his official robe."

He hurried out, bowed to the governor and said: "It is a great honour to have the governor calling in person."

Yang took his arm in a friendly fashion: "I know you announced that you're not seeing any officials in Hangzhou. But we have worked together for many years in the past. Maybe you'll make an exception."

Hu hastened to reply: "I ought to have been in touch long ago. But the documents have been piling up like a mountain and I'm still trying to put them into shape. Please forgive my neglect."

They walked arm-in-arm into the reception hall, where a maid brought tea and pastries. After waving the attendants away, Hu said: "To tell you the truth, I have been concentrating my efforts on studying literature and know very little about the subtleties and twists of law cases. I hope you'll enlighten me."

Yang replied: "You're too polite. I practically know next to nothing about criminal law."

Hu studied Yang for a while. "You have many meritorious deeds to your credit. When I was reading Yang Naiwu's case just now, I kept wondering to myself, how could a person as astute and experienced as you have trusted, without evidence, the careless condemnation made by the county magistrate and the prefect? It has caused such consternation among your Zhejiang colleagues, that they reported their feelings to the imperial court."

Yang sighed deeply: "As a person who has lived in the capital for so long, you can hardly imagine the complicated situation in the provinces. The saying goes: 'On entering a country, ask about its customs.' To shut yourself away and refuse to see your colleagues in order to keep yourself above reproach — well, that may be possible if you're just writing reports. But it is far more difficult handling practical matters." He shook his head to stress his point.

Hu smiled: "To study diligently and become an official, one needs to be extremely 'careful'. One false move and your official hat is confiscated. There are discrepancies in the investigation made by the Yuhang magistrate and Hangzhou prefect. The date of the murder, the autopsy, the confessions of the two involved — none of them fit. Yet you and the provincial judge and treasurer overlooked all that and did not correct the mistakes. That is very careless. Very careless."

Yang laughed: "Do you know who the literary chancellor was when Yang Naiwu passed the provincial examination? Who removed his title of *juren* based on the reports sent by Yuhang County and the Hangzhou prefect?"

Yang continued: "You must know that the former literary chancellor is no other than your father-in-law. When the three provincial authorities — the governor, the judge and the treasurer — were asked to carry out a joint investigation of the case, your father-in-law already had Yang Naiwu's title removed. All I did was follow procedures."

Hu's hand twitched and he knocked over a teacup. He rose in a fluster and stood before a painting of a landscape.

Yang sipped some tea and went on: "To tell you the truth, I had originally intended to right the wrong done to Yang Naiwu. But after weighing the matter over and over again, I refrained from doing so. For although I would win fame, your father-in-law's high post, due to his connection with the Yuhang magistrate and Hangzhou prefect, would be in danger. I heard your father-in-law gave you a lot of help in your studies and promotion. I don't think you should forget his kindness and not want to repay him."

Hu stamped his foot in frustration. "Why did the Empress Dowager have to choose me to do the job?"

Yang replied: "The Empress Dowager always puts the right person in the right job. She knows you are originally from the south, and not from Hunan, so you cannot be suspected of trying to cover up for the Hunanese working here. She also knows that your appointment was on the repeated recommendations by your father-in-law and by me, the governor of Zhejiang who originally came from Hunan."

Hu was confused: "If that being the case..." He lowered his head and when he raised it again, he found Yang gone. He had not even bidden him farewell. Hu was more perturbed than ever.

As Yang mounted his sedan chair, he tossed a large red envelope onto the ground and ordered that it be delivered to the literary chancellor to read and then to tear up.

The more Hu thought, the more on tenterhooks he became. He walked into his study and fixed his gaze at the couplet hanging on the wall: "Peruse books by Sages, and handle matters of the state."

Outside, his military secretary took the envelope and pushed open the door.

Hu snapped: "Go away."

But the secretary said: "My lord, the governor went off in a huff and tossed this envelope out of the sedan chair."

It was addressed to Hu and the senders were Judge Kuai, Prefect Chen and a hundred other officials. Hu opened the envelope and saw a money order for three hundred thousand taels of silver. His eyes widened in disbelief.

He heard his military secretary say: "The governor said you're to tear it up after reading it."

Hu, his mind in a whirl, began to tear, but stopped. His hands trembled and his eyes dilated. He was unsure....

The secretary glanced at the money order and said: "Let me send it back."

Hu shook his head: "We can't do that."

The military secretary gave a wry smile and asked for a long leave.

Hu answered: "I have come to my post only recently and have not started yet on Yang Naiwu's case. Why do you ask for leave?"

The secretary answered: "My ancestors and family are from Shaoxing, Zhejiang Province. When I came here I promised my parents and our clan leader that I would one day return and have our ancestral temple renovated. In these three weeks, since you came, you asked me to reject all gifts from your relatives and friends who want favours from you. Am I to suppose that you brought ten thousand taels of property with you?"

Hu said: "I'm as poor as anything."

The secretary said in a helpless tone: "People say, one becomes an official either by fame or wealth. But those working under you have neither. It seems I have to look for a better job with prospects."

Hu sighed: "You must know the difficult position I am in. Reverse the verdict or not to reverse the verdict — both are difficult. The only thing I can do is return to the capital and plead incompetence and ask the Empress Dowager to replace me."

"Then your ten years of hard study and twenty

years of waiting for such a post will be wasted," said the secretary.

Hu said despondently: "I have no idea how to go about solving this dilemma."

The secretary sat himself down beside the desk and said: "A teacher in my home town claims that all good ideas come from Zhejiang and the best of all comes from Shaoxing. My uncle can conjure up all sorts of ideas and then asks my opinion. So let me think of some plan and you accept the money and forget about public opinion."

"How can I do that?" asked Hu.

"In the first place, you must not take part in any interrogation. You must not use torture. Do not give cause to the Zhejiang officials to conspire against you. Use the ancient trick of looking at details but do not be too specific about the exact nature of your investigation. That will keep your superiors and subordinates satisfied and give you time...."

What clever ruse was it that made the literary chancellor happy?

We'll find out when Yang Naiwu and Little Cabbage were brought to trial again.

It was being held in the governor's *yamen* which was packed with people who wanted to see the new literary chancellor sent by the Empress Dowager herself, to reopen Yang Naiwu's case.

Among the audience was Yang Naiwu's sister Shuying, his wife Cuifeng and his old servant Chen Laode. It was an exceptional scene: no torture instruments and the court runners no longer shouting to intimidate the prisoners. Everyone was impressed.

The two prisoners were brought in. Unlike before

when the court was filled with officials, the only ones present were the Literary Chancellor Hu Ruilan, Governor Yang Changjun, Judge Kuai, Prefect Chen and Magistrate Liu.

In a kindly voice Hu said: "Yours is a case which concerns public morals. You have retracted your confessions many times. As a newly appointed literary chancellor to this province, I have no connections with the officials who interrogated you formerly. I have gone through your confessions and find that really the crux of the matter is whether you two committed adultery. I have decided that a blood test will decide the issue."

To decide a case on such a ridiculous test made Yang Naiwu answer in shocked disbelief: "Stupid I may be, but even I know a blood test can only decide a relationship between parent and child, not between a man and woman."

But shaking his head, Hu said: "The books state: The *yin* and *yang* of men and women desiring each other match their blood — mix and make them inseparable like glue or paint."

"Ha," said Naiwu, scornfully, "old wives tales, how can an imperial commissioner trust that?"

The military secretary intervened: "I know you have a sharp pen and a clever turn of phrase. That's why his excellency does not believe in your confession. He has to use a blood test. The fact you fear this blood test shows you are guilty."

Xiugu grasped this thin thread of hope: "I'm willing to have the test," she said. She turned to Naiwu. "In the years we have known each other, our behaviour has been beyond reproach. The test can prove that we are innocent."

Naiwu had no alternative but to agree.

A bowl of water and two long silver needles were brought in. The cangues were removed from their necks and one of their sleeves rolled up. Hu knew that the blood test was just a red herring to fool the court. It was obvious that over a hundred officials wanted Yang Naiwu dead. If he saved his life, he would have to remove the official posts of a hundred, including that of his father-in-law, whereas if he took the opposite course, a hundred or so officials would be in his debt. As he pondered over his dilemma, blood was drawn from the two prisoners and it was mixed in the bowl of water.

The military secretary announced in a loud voice: "The blood of the man and woman mix well."

Hu and Yang smiled at each other as he shouted across to the two: "Your blood clings together. They cannot be separated."

Xiugu cried out in despair and Naiwu shouted: "It's ridiculous!"

Chen Laode said to Shuying and Cuifeng: "They have tricked us. That silver needle is very suspicious."

Hu ordered the court to be adjourned.

Governor Yang remarked to Judge Kuai and Prefect Chen: "The commissioner is worthy of the Empress Dowager's trust."

Liu Xitong and Chen wiped the cold sweat from their foreheads while Kuai stuck up a thumb.

But people in the audience wondered whether a blood test could really determine adultery.

All during the proceedings, Liu Xitong's wife had been kneeling before the Buddha praying with all her might. Secretary Zhao entered posthaste followed by

Shedding Blood in the Yamen 161

Liu Xitong's concubine and his son Liu Zihe.

Secretary Zhao first kowtowed repeatedly to the memorial tablets of Liu's ancestors, downed two cups of tea, filled his pipe which the concubine lit for him, before he slapped his thigh and told the expectant group the outcome of the court session.

"Fantastic! It was fantastic! Thanks to the secret blessing by the Liu family's ancestors, the commissioner made them take a blood test and what do you think? Their blood mixed together. That is iron-clad evidence."

Liu Zihe scratched his head, while the concubine said what a wonderful man he was. Mrs. Liu ordered her son to kowtow before his ancestors' tablets in gratitude for their intervention.

Zhao handed back his pipe to the concubine and said: "But..."

"But what?" asked Mrs. Liu.

"I think four thousand dollars is too little."

Mrs. Liu was about to protest but her son whispered to her: "Give him more please."

She slapped him across the face. "It was all your wrong doing!" she exclaimed. "We'll be bankrupt before this case is over. You won't get another copper from me."

Zhao fell silent. The concubine said pacifyingly: "Let's wait until the magistrate returns, then we'll see."

Mrs. Liu glared at her.

Having placed so much hope on the new commissioner, Yang Naiwu's family were desperately disappointed over his handling of the case. News spread throughout the city of Hangzhou that the blood test had proved Naiwu and Xiugu had committed adultery.

Soon after, Naiwu's mother-in-law came to remove her daughter from the Yang household. Shuying was unable to make any excuse, saying: "Two years ago I suggested that Cuifeng was still young and as the marriage had not been consummated, she should return home. She shouldn't waste her future like this ... but all officials cover up for each other and with the prospects so poor, Naiwu has little chance of being cleared." Then she turned to Cuifeng and continued: "I don't want our misfortunes to fall on your family. You should divorce Naiwu and find another husband."

But Cuifeng was adamant: "Once I married into the Yang family, I shall remain even as a ghost of the Yangs."

Her mother was unable to dissuade her and her heart bled for her daughter's misery.

The death cell was grim and dark. Though Naiwu was in chains with a cangue round his neck and dirty and dishevelled, his eyes were piercingly alive and bright. By a shaft of light which shone dimly through a tiny window, he was writing a couplet on the dirty wall of his cell:

"Suddenly, a provincial graduate becomes a criminal a shame for scholarly learning.
The provincial authorities are in truth torturers
— Naiwu is dying."

He tossed the brush onto the ground and cried out in despair:

"Oh heavens. Is there no upright official in the Qing court?"

The cell door swung open and his wife and sister entered.

He was surprised to see his wife and said bitterly: "When the document arrives from the capital, I shall be beheaded. You should find another husband."

Weeping, Cuifeng replied: "I now belong to the Yang family, dead or alive."

He shook his head: "The sooner I am dead the better for all concerned."

His sister said: "If you should die, your wrong cannot be righted."

"Then I'll leave a most intriguing case for posterity," he said.

Shuying said: "I've decided to travel to the capital to petition the Board of Punishments."

"But it is over three thousand *li* away and it's freezing cold in the north. Besides, civilians are not allowed to complain against an official. If they insist they must first lie on a board of steel spikes. They'd be more dead than alive after that."

They pressurized Naiwu to agree to write out the petition for them and they would both take it and travel to the capital.

Shuying persuaded the warder to smuggle in an inkstone and brush, saying: "My mother often wakes up in the night fearing her son's safety. Let him write to her to assure her all is well. Then she will be able to sleep at night." She removed a jade bangle from her wrist and gave it to him.

"You'd better be quick," he said taking the bangle. "I know your mother died years ago!"

Shuying bent down and Naiwu spread the paper on her back, while Cuifeng ground the inkstick into the stone. By the time he had finished the petition, sweat stood out on his brow. Shuying placed the paper inside her jacket and they stepped out of the cell.

As they left, Naiwu told them: "I still have misgivings, but on your way to the capital, stop over at Tangxi and look up a man called White-browed Li and ask him to look over the petition. He writes better than I do and my life depends on this."

To Lodge A Petition in the Capital

ALL the provincial graduates and scholars in Hangzhou had disapproved of the way Literary Chancellor Hu had conducted the interrogation. No one believed blood tests could determine adultery, yet the court convened by the imperial commissioner and the three top local authorities had carried out such a test.

The Kong brothers, Naiwu's best friends and a few of the gentry were discussing the discredited outcome. The second son of the Kongs began: "I never expected the imperial commissioner to be such a stupid person. It's a disgrace."

His father agreed and heaved a long sigh. "I heard Naiwu wrote a couplet on his prison wall."

"Yes," said Ding, another provincial graduate and he recited the verse:

"*Suddenly, a provincial graduate becomes a criminal a shame for scholarly learning.*
The provincial authorities are in truth torturers
— Naiwu is dying."

Father Kong said: "Well written! A wonderful couplet!"

Ding replied: "I never thought a scholar like the literary chancellor could be so hard on another scholar."

The elder son of the Kongs recited a poem in which the hidden meaning implied criticism of the Qing court:

"The night is so long, when will daylight come?
Will the murky waters of the Qiantang become clear?"*

"Stop!" said one of the scholars. "The last word in those lines is forbidden. You will be arrested if others get to know about it."

"Never mind," said the second son, "we're all friends here. What a pity the country no longer belongs to the Han nation."

The elder son rejoined: "Hangzhou doesn't belong to the Manchus (Qing Dynasty) either. It belongs to the Hunan warlords and governor Yang Changjun."

They all fell silent. The stillness was broken by a servant announcing the arrival of Naiwu's sister Shuying. After the formal greetings were made she told them she was on her way to the capital to petition the Board of Punishments. "I'm hoping against hope," she said, "I will kneel there with the petition on my back and plead for Naiwu's life."

The Kongs and the other scholars were conscience-stricken. All they had done was voice their discontent and disapproval while Shuying — a woman — had the courage and loyalty to plead for her brother's life at the risk of her own.

They plucked up courage and decided also to pen a petition and sign their names, thereby sharing the risk.

The elder Kong suddenly thought of something else. "You need more help, Miss Yang," he said. "The vice-

---

*"Clear" has the same sound in Chinese as Qing of the Qing Dynasty.

minister of the Board of Punishments is Mr. Xia Tongshan, go to him when you reach the capital. He might get the case reopened."

Shuying was dubious. "Through your recommendation, I once worked as his mother's hairdresser many years ago. I would not want to jeopardise his career."

Old man Kong reassured her: "I'll put my name down first on this petition. It will be my responsibility. Even if it should wreck his career, he would not blame you, it will be me." He added: "Your trip to the capital concerns six lives."

Shuying shook her head in disbelief.

"Just think of it," said old man Kong. "If the verdict is not reversed Naiwu will be beheaded, Little Cabbage dismembered first and then beheaded. Sangu, her sister-in-law, is too young to take care of herself, and how long would his wife live after this? Add to this Miss Yang herself and her son. Well that amounts to six lives."

They read through the petition and old man Kong thought each word had been carefully chosen and was very convincing.

"'When a wrong is not righted, people have no security.' These two lines," he said, "are a variation of 'If evil ministers are not removed, the state will have no peace.' Too true. Let me put my name down first, and you, sub-prefect, be the next to sign."

"We should get more influential people to sign," suggested the sub-prefect. "It might work better."

"You're right," said old man Kong. "A bundle of firewood is hard to snap. And more fuel makes a bigger fire."

Shuying was heartened by their concern but she wondered about the long trip and whether disaster or good fortune waited at the end.

Early the following day, Shuying and Cuifeng went to the Temple of the City God to burn incense. Buddhist devotees were praying before lighted red candles and joss-sticks in front of the idol. The two women knelt down and shook a bamboo tube until a stick fell out. They showed it to an old monk who interpreted the oracle as if it came from the idol itself:

*"When peach trees blossom, the outcome shows
Spring leaves and willow flowers with meaning laden.
Examine oneself, examine people and examine good
  fortune.
Hope will be yours when autumn winds waft open
  the osmanthus."*

The monk asked: "Do you want to know if you'll have a son or is it something else?"

Shuying answered: "I want to know if the wrong sentence on my brother can be righted."

The old monk thought for a while and then said: "When peach trees blossom, the outcome shows. Things will take a turn for the better next spring when peach trees blossom. But you won't see the results until autumn when the osmanthus are in bloom."

Cuifeng asked: "Could you tell me when he'll be able to come home?"

He gave another oracle saying:

*"Destined for life, yet parted by space,
Long distances are covered over cloudy mountains*

*The date of return of the beloved
Is when breezes rustle amid lotus leaves."*

Cuifeng smiled: "The lotus blooms before the osmanthus."

Shuying's health was giving cause for concern, so they went to see an old physician who felt her pulse and asked questions. When he discovered they were relatives of Yang Naiwu he offered to help them, by introducing them to his former superior, the owner of the Hu Qingyu Pharmacy and well-known in Hangzhou. He had once been in charge of the commissariat for a warlord of Hunan and owing to his expertise had been given the title of second rank official. He took the two women to Hu's residence where they sat in silence as Hu Xueyan drew on his water pipe and a provincial graduate named Zhou paced the floor giving his interpretation of the case. "Something is very fishy about this," he said. "From the provincial governor down to the Yuhang magistrate, they seem bent on persecuting them. Even the commissioner is in cahoots with them."

"Does that mean there is not one upright official in Hangzhou?" Shuying asked.

All eyes turned to the old pharmacist, who, choked by the smoke from his water pipe, began to cough. A maid quickly brought a spittoon. He slammed his water pipe on the table and said: "If you, a young lady, can fight for your brother's life and is prepared to travel thousands of *li*, how can I stand by with folded arms?"

He turned to the old physician: "Mr. Huang,

please take the two ladies to the accountant and get two hundred taels of silver for their travelling expenses."

The graduate Zhou said: "In support of the Zhejiang scholars who courageously put their names to the petition, I have also signed it. All the teachers and students of the Imperial Academy in Hangzhou will be asked to sign too."

With the money and the petition signed by Hangzhou's worthy citizens, the two women started on their long journey. On their way, they visited White-browed Li as Naiwu had suggested, and asked him to look over Naiwu's written petition.

"It's a bit strong," he exclaimed. "I always knew Naiwu had a pungent style. It is well written but it should be milder in tone. He writes for example: 'In the south, the sun and moon disappear. In the country, the people see no justice.' Excellent sentences which reflect his feelings but it will not help him. On the contrary, it might have the reverse effect. I shall make a slight change. I'll write: 'In the south, the sun and moon disappear, but in the country, the people see justice.'"

Shuying saw the point. "You are a great scholar," she said. "The slight change is important."

With the improved petition and the petition signed by the Hangzhou scholars, the two women continued their long arduous journey.

Prodding the Prince with Wit

IT was a trying journey for the two women as they travelled from Yuhang to the capital Beijing. It took five months by boat and a hundred days by land — almost three thousand *li* before they finally reached their destination.

The majestic splendour of the Forbidden City, with its golden tiles, rose before them as they wearily walked through the city gate.

They found a small inn, and then went to call on the vice-minister of the Board of Punishments, Xia Tongshan. Shuying had once studied with his daughter and had often dressed his mother's hair for her. Being a filial son, Xia treated the Yang family well.

They first paid their respects to the old mother and as Shuying began dressing her hair, as in older times, the daughter-in-law of the house and the grandchildren also entered the room to pay their respects to the old lady.

Shuying had disclosed the reason why she had come to Beijing and old lady Xia cautioned her about the way she should approach the matter. "To lodge a complaint against a government official, one must first lay on a board of steel spikes. Only two persons have lain on a board of steel spikes to lodge complaints," she said. "And you are the first to complain about over a hundred officials in Zhejiang. This is not a minor affair, wait until my son comes home. I'll ask him to think of a way, so don't go to the Board of Punishments yet."

When Xia Tongshan arrived he went straight into his mother's room to pay his respects. Shuying hid behind a screen. After the formal greetings were over, old lady Xia questioned him about Yang Naiwu's case.

With furrowed brow, Xia said that nothing could be changed as the emperor had verified the decision to remove Naiwu's title of provincial graduate so he could be executed for the crime he had been found guilty of.

Unable to remain silent Shuying emerged from behind the screen and flung herself down before Xia Tongshan. "Please hold back the orders for a few days at least," she pleaded. "My brother is innocent. Even if the emperor's decision cannot be rescinded, he still has to finalize the decision. Tomorrow I will go to the Board of Punishments and strike the drum at the gate of the courtroom."

"Could you not keep the orders back for one day, my son?" asked the old lady.

Xia lowered his head. "I dare not disobey the emperor," he said.

"What is the first priority of a court official?" demanded the old lady.

"Respect the emperor and place the people first."

"Place the people first indeed! Tell me then, is Yang Naiwu wronged or not? You are vice-minister of the Board of Punishments. Yet you fail to minister to the rights of the people and your country. I have failed in my duty as a mother, if you do not know what is right and what is wrong, or cannot distinguish black from white. How can I face your dead father in the future?'' Tears rolled down her cheeks.

His mother's tears brought her son down to his knees. His wife and children and the maids also followed suit. Regretting the trouble she had caused, Shuying also went down on her knees.

The old lady pulled Shuying up: "I was only giving that unfilial son of mine a piece of my mind."

Her daughter-in-law gave a meaningful glance at her eight-year-old son who was the apple of his grandmother's eye. Only he could get them out of this predicament today. Still kneeling, the astute child moved over to his grandmother and placed his hands on her lap.

"Don't be upset, granny, father is sure to do what he can for the Yang family."

The old lady laughed at the grown-up way her grandson spoke. She told them all to rise.

Xia Tongshan promised to go to see the minister of the Board of Punishments, Sang Chunrong, immediately.

Shuying handed him the petition written and signed by all the Zhejiang scholars.

"This will greatly help the case," he said.

"What will you do if Mr. Sang refuses to help?" asked his mother.

"Then I'll resign and plant fields as an ordinary citizen," he said.

She nodded: "I'm proud of you, my son," she said. In response to Shuying's fears over his future, she answered: "I'd rather he loses his position than your brother his life."

At their small inn, Shuying and Cuifeng were memorizing their petition. Cuifeng begged that she be allowed to present it but Shuying was adamant. "For three generations the Yang family has had only one male descendant. If blessed by Buddha, Naiwu will have his wrong redressed and be released. You will then have to shoulder the solemn responsibility of carrying on the family line. This is my filial responsibility. There is just one thing else I want you to do. Take care of my son when I am gone and he becomes an orphan."

To save Naiwu, both women were prepared to go through the ordeal at the Board of Punishments even if it meant climbing a mountain of knives or plunging into a sea of fire.

A wooden memorial arch standing on massive stone bases, with golden characters inscribed on a blue background at the top, spanned the wide street which ran straight through the heart of Beijing. In the capital, no official was allowed to go through in a pompous way like beating gongs to clear the way or carrying banners stating his rank. Without special permission from the emperor, an official was not allowed to be carried in a sedan chair. He could only ride a horse or travel in a carriage.

The minister of the Board of Punishments, Sang Chunrong, a first-rank official, had the privilege of a sedan chair. His eyes half-closed, he looked extremely solemn and complacent. Two runners before the sedan chair carried red gauze lanterns inscribed with the characters: "Minister of the Board of Punishments". Guards on horseback rode behind. Suddenly a woman dashed out from the side and ignoring the runners and the whips prostrated herself in front of the sedan chair.

She cried out: "I want to lodge a complaint!"

The sedan chair halted and Sang opened his eyes: "What is she complaining about?"

Shuying cried: "I complain about the officials in Zhejiang from the governor down to the county magistrate who have conspired to frame my brother. He has been in prison for three whole years." Sang Chunrong was shocked. To reopen the case countless officials would be involved. It was much too risky. "Chase her away," he ordered.

She was dragged into a side lane and left shrieking to the sky: "I'm wronged and my brother is wronged!"

At almost the same time as Shuying's demonstration, a German-made carriage arrived at Xia Tongshan's residence. Four eunuchs helped Prince Chun, father of the emperor, to alight.

He had a slight limp, but he was dressed in a sable gown and his pigtail was over a foot long. He had many interesting ornaments hanging on his gown — a gold watch, a snuff bottle and other curios... Wang Xin, a censor, followed him out. He was in his thirties, fair complexioned, and the two would often visit Xia to play chess and drink wine. As the prince and his entourage was about to enter Xia's study, they heard the angry voice of Xia as he banged on the desk. "Tongshan is normally a good natured man, so why is he...?" He wondered. Then they heard Xia's secretary say: "What has this world turned to? I'm really sick and tired of it all!"

Chun wanted to go in and placate his friend's anger, but Wang Xin suggested they listen a bit more.

"To extract a confession by punishment and no intelligent man intervenes. Have all the scholars in the country died?"

The voice of Xia's secretary was heard. "Please don't be upset. If Your Excellency feels it is beyond your power to help, you can enlist your old friends among the imperial relatives."

Prince Chun nudged Wang Xin: "Now we'll be rounded in." Then they heard Xia continue: "The only people I know are fair-weather friends."

Prince Chun was angry when he heard this and turned to leave but Wang Xin stopped him: "Don't take any notice of things said in anger."

In the study, Xia's former secretary, Li Ruizhai, now his son's tutor, a man with grey hair and wearing a fur gown and black jacket, his pigtail as thin as a rat's tail, was laughing up his sleeve. It was his idea to stage this act with Xia. He said: "But we must still make every possible effort and doctor the dead horse as if it were still alive, as the saying goes."

Xia answered: "But the emperor has already decided. Even Prince Chun can't do anything now."

Li Ruizhai said: "Prince Chun ... he is the emperor's father ... He can still bombard like a big gun."

Xia replied that to right the wrong of a civilian, even the big gun wouldn't work.

Prince Chun's eyes rolled with rage.

"What about Censor Wang, then?" asked the tutor.

"Shuying claims there are no upright officials in the Forbidden City," Xia replied.

Prince Chun's whiskers bristled: "I'm a big gun and you're the small one. Let the two guns bombard together!" He kicked open the door.

Xia quickly made a formal bow.

Prince Chun remained silent with a stony face. He moved over to the desk, pounded it and cried: "I'm sick and tired of it all!"

Xia wanted to know what was wrong.

"We were listening outside the door," said the prince.

Xia said: "We were discussing the case of Yang Naiwu."

Prince Chun was intrigued and asked for more details.

Xia related the whole story, the original report from Zhejiang which was full of contradictions. The petitions of Shuying, and details of all the nine interrogations and sentences made by the county, the prefecture, the provincial judge and provincal governor. "All the officials have covered up for each other and treated this man's life as if it were a straw."

"This is really outrageous," cried Wang Xin.

Prince Chun said: "Nine interrogations and nine sentences? In that case all the officials in Zhejiang are involved."

Wang Xin was familiar with the recent history of Zhejiang Province. So he said: "Officials there are all outstanding generals and officers of the Hunan troops who have been amassing power, and their henchmen are hard to control. Since the death of Emperor Tongzhi, the south has been at war for many years. The Zhejiang people are already angry over the handling of Yang Naiwu's case. If a careless move is made, trouble might arise. The prince should give the matter careful consideration."

Although the prince enjoyed the good things of life — flowers, wine, chess and cricket fights — he was quite familiar with the factional struggles among ministers and officials.

He began to think what measures he could take.

Xia said: "Yang Naiwu's sister and wife have come a long way to the capital to lodge a complaint. They have also brought a petition signed by distinguished personages of Zhejiang and the entire imperial academy."

He gave the petition to the prince. "To reopen the case and right the wrong, we need to have the prisoners removed to the capital to be reinterrogated here."

The prince pulled out his watch hanging at his waist. "I'll go to the palace right away and see the Empress Dowager."

Surrounded by his runners, the minister of the Board of Punishments arrived at the gate of his residence. As soon as he stepped down, Shuying rushed forward crying out again: "I have a complaint to make."

"What a nerve this woman has," he raged.

Before she could be removed she clutched his gown and pleaded: "Please don't be angry, Your Excellency. I have come three thousand *li* to see you. I hope an upright official as you are will be able to right the wrong done to my brother."

He waved his men away as they tried to drag Shuying back. He had originally been a good official but now, getting on in years, officialdom had worn away his good intentions and he was not as conscientious as he used to be. He just wanted to drift along with the tide and get by. He took Shuying's petition, read it and found it involved half the officials of Zhejiang.

He gave a deep sigh: "To complain against an official is forbidden but since you are a woman and doing it for your brother, I'll overlook it."

Shuying in despair cried out: "I had placed all my hopes on you being a just and upright man but I see now all officials are birds of the same feather. You cover up for each other and distort the law for your own ends."

Sang flew into a rage: "Brazen hussy!" His runners moved up to arrest her.

She pulled out a long sharp knife and cried: "If you refuse to accept my petition, I shall kill myself on the spot!"

The minister had long lost any moral fibre because of years of bureaucracy and told his runners to remove her.

The scene was witnessed by Prince Chun who stopped his carriage and came out. "Who is this woman?" he asked.

"I am Yang Shuying," she answered. "We have endured a great injustice."

Seeing the petition in her hand, he turned to Sang and said: "I hope you have accepted it."

The prince smiled at Shuying: "You have approached the right man. Mr. Sang is a first-rank official. He has the power to kill corrupt officials in the provinces. He used to be just as upright as the legendary Judge Bao."

The prince's innuendoes made Sang go red. "I do not live up to your compliments," he said.

"What about this petition?" the prince asked.

"I'm afraid the emperor has already given his opinion. I wonder if the Empress Dowager..." Sang hazarded.

"I'm going to see her now," Prince Chun answered.

Lying on A Board of Spikes

THE Palace of Everlasting Spring was the living quarters of the Empress Dowager. It was a resplendent building with exquisitely carved and painted eaves in green and gold.

A horizontal placard which hung under the eaves of the principal hall read "Culture the Heart and the Mind." On the two red pillars hung a couplet:

*"A moon at the side of the Highest Supreme
Receives reverence from all the stars;
Thunderous hails to the sovereign
As foretold from the west."*

The walls of the corridor leading to the hall were covered with scenes from *A Dream of Red Mansions*. Opposite was a decorated performing stage. The Empress Dowager sat facing the stage. In her Manchu court dress and laden with jewellery, she was the very picture of elegance and grace. Behind her were the court ladies and beside her was the chief eunuch, Li Lianying.

Prince Chun sat at one side. Two magicians were giving a performance. One of them waved his long sleeve over an empty bowl and it was instantly filled with water. The court ladies and the eunuchs marvelled while Prince Chun exclaimed: "Fantastic!"

But the Empress Dowager remained unmoved.

When a young actress reached into the bowl, her dainty fingers lifted out a lotus bud which gradually opened its petals sending a fragrance through the hall. Again the audience gasped in surprise and Prince Chun chuckled saying: "This is really something!" The Empress Dowager allowed herself a faint glimmer of a smile.

The performers came before the Empress Dowager and kneeling down said: "There are characters written in the heart of the flower," and asked her to look. Her curiosity getting the better of her, she rose from her seat and looked in the bowl where the lotus flower revealed the message: "A long, long life to you!"

The assemblage all went down on their knees and kowtowed three times: "A long, long life to the Old Buddha," they repeated.

Prince Chun stood before her in a very respectful manner. "The gods from Penglai Fairy Island must be wishing you a happy fortieth birthday."

Now in a good mood, the Empress Dowager presented two small gold ingots to the performers.

Seeing her change of mood, Prince Chun lost no time in saying: "When Your Majesty gave a general amnesty to celebrate your fortieth birthday, the people acclaimed your benevolence, believing you love them like your own children. Only a recent provincial graduate, Yang Naiwu, is still under sentence for something he did not do. People are saying he has not received the same treatment."

The Empress Dowager was displeased and asked what the officials in Zhejiang were doing about it. Prince Chun answered: "The Hunan armymen have stayed there too long. If they should expand their power they will be harder to control. The south has always been restless. Now Yang Naiwu has been in prison for three years. The gentry and the imperial academy are unsettled and have sent a joint petition to the court. If this case is not settled, the people might rebel.'' He took out the petition and presented it to the Empress Dowager.

She answered: "Let Yang Naiwu live if possible."

He thanked her but reminded her that his execution had already been approved and the Board of Punishments did not dare to reinterrogate.

The Empress Dowager demanded: "Why not, if he is wronged?"

Prince Chun replied: "Of course. I shall obey the orders of the Empress Dowager."

Just one sentence from the Empress Dowager and it became possible to punish the local officials in Zhejiang, and the overbearing Hunan armymen. But the cunning Empress Dowager knew it made sense, because by doing this she was able to remove a hidden peril and consolidate her ruling powers.

An excited Prince Chun hopped out of his carriage and ran into the residence of Sang Chunrong, minister of the Board of Punishments and told him that the Empress Dowager had ordered him to reopen the case of Yang Naiwu.

"I shall obey orders," said Sang while Prince Chun declared: "And I'll come and see how you handle it."

The *yamen* of the Board of Punishments was an imposing building. Fierce court runners brandished whips and weapons to intimidate onlookers and drive the crowds away from the gate.

A board for receiving complaints was hung outside the gate to the accompaniment of drums and trumpets. Yang Shuying pushed her way through the crowd, followed closely by her sister-in-law, Cuifeng, both eager to get to the board first. Shuying pushed Cuifeng down and ran forward to take the board and carry it into the *yamen*.

Once inside, Shuying showed no fear despite the many torture instruments displayed round the hall.

Over the courtroom was a notice which read: "Severe punishment, mirror-like justice".

Murderous-looking soldiers and policemen lined the courtroom leaving a narrow path which led to a strange-looking bench covered with steel spikes which glittered under the light.

This was the spike-board which civilians in feudal times were required to lie on before they could complain against officials. In the two hundred years of Qing rule, Shuying was only the third person to use it.

The minister of the Board of Punishments, Sang Chunrong, sat on his official seat. The vice-minister, Xia Tongshan, sat by his side. In a side chamber, Prince Chun and Wang Xin were seated. The prince in a sable gown and fur cap with a piece of white jade embedded in the front was dressed as if he was at the theatre.

To the sound of drums and gongs, Shuying carried the permit board in front of her and walked fearlessly through the narrow path towards the bench of steel spikes.

She handed her petition to a clerk and then cried: "Please give me justice, upright judge!" and threw herself onto the spikes.

Prince Chun was overcome and said to Wang Xin: "If I had known about this board of spikes we should have exempted her from it."

Wang Xin replied: "That we could not do. It is the law of the Qing Dynasty."

Four court runners carried the board with Shuying impaled upon it into the courtroom. Her face deathly pale, she was close to losing consciousness. Her limbs felt as if they were being torn by dogs. She let out a slight groan which touched the hearts of the people in the court. Sang himself had to steel himself to call out: "What outrageous woman dares to make false charges against officials?"

Shuying said in a low voice: "Everything I shall say is the truth."

Sang fixed his eyes upon her and said: "You've got to recite your petition. It will not be accepted if you make one mistake."

Blood trickled down from the bench to the floor. Shuying was in excruciating pain but a voice within her kept saying: "Not a word wrong, not a word wrong..." Her mind cleared and she raised her head from the board and the words Naiwu wrote in his petition seemed to appear before her.

"I am Yang Shuying from Yuhang, Zhejiang Province. I lived with my brother Yang Naiwu who studied hard. He passed the imperial examination at provincial level and became a *juren* and got married at that time. Our family was celebrating these two happy events when the magistrate of Yuhang falsely accused him of having an affair with the maid-servant Xiugu and murdering her husband. He was framed by the magistrate of Yuhang who harboured a grudge against him. He was tortured into making a false confession...."

Shuying recited word by word, her voice growing stronger as the agony and anger which she had harboured for so long at last could be expressed. It touched the hearts of the people present.

Sang followed closely each word of the written petition while Prince Chun, saddened, produced a snuff bottle and took a hard sniff.

Enduring the pain and fighting back dizziness, Shuying recited to the end, taking care to utter every word correctly. Vice-minister Xia and Prince Chun uttered sighs of relief.

When the court runners moved to help Shuying up from the board she said she would not budge unless Minister Sang accepted her petition. "I'll bleed to death on this board."

Only when he agreed did Shuying allow herself to be helped up. She said: "I have another favour to ask Your Excellency. Please make sure all the prisoners are to be interrogated by the Board of Punishments and not by the officials of Zhejiang who will cover up for each other."

Minister Sang looked at Xia who in turn looked at Prince Chun who nodded his head and patted his chest.

Reassured, Sang said: "Your request is granted. I'll report to the emperor."

Shuying kowtowed and then she was carried out of the *yamen* where a waiting Cuifeng dressed her wounds.

Inside Prince Chun heaved a sigh of relief: "Now!"

Wang Xin said: "I'm still not sure if the case can be redressed. Among the hundred or so officials in

Zhejiang involved in this case, you only need one to befriend the commissioner, he could kill a few witnesses and steal one of the files, then it would always remain a mystery, even if the emperor gives consent to reopen the case. Let me go to Zhejiang, and I'll bring all the prisoners here and every single sheet of the files."

Prince Chun patted his shoulder: "What a man! You've volunteered!"

A boat sailed in the Yuhang River. Dressed in ordinary clothes, Wang Xin sat enjoying the scenery of the south. As it was already early winter the scene looked a little desolate. The boatman, named Ah Yi, in his fifties, was a pleasant talkative man. "You seem to be a scholar, sir," he said.

Wang smiled nodding.

"Have you passed the imperial examination at prefectural level?"

He shook his head.

"What are you doing in Yuhang?"

"To buy silk floss," answered Wang.

"I see," said the boatman. "You've failed your exams and have turned to business. In my opinion a business does not bring in much money. You're better off being an official."

"How can I be an official if I haven't passed the prefectural examination?" Wang Xin asked.

"That's no problem," answered the boatman, "you can buy a post with money, like the magistrate of Yuhang."

"Does he have a good reputation?" Wang Xin asked.

"His nickname is 'Black Lacquered Lantern'."

"What does that mean?"

"A lantern that is covered with a layer of black lacquer," said the boatman.

"As dark as can be," laughed Wang Xin.

Ah Yi let out a sigh. "This Black Lacquered Lantern has broken up the family of my old customer Yang Naiwu." The boatman, encouraged by Wang Xin, related the details and then fished out an old account book with yellow pages. "Look," he said, "I recorded the dates here of when Yang Naiwu left for Hangzhou and when I took him back...."

The boat drew up to the bank and the boatman took Wang Xin and his servant to the gate of Yang Naiwu's house in Clarification Lane.

A young man came out of the gate and Wang Xin asked if it was the home of Naiwu. He was told that the house had been sold when Naiwu was imprisoned.

Then Ah Yi took Wang Xin to Peaceful Lane where they found the former home of Xiugu, dilapidated and the mulberry garden behind it deserted.

Wang Xin said to himself: "Things are not clarified in Clarification Lane and not peaceful in Peaceful Lane."

A wooden door opened and a little girl of about ten threw out a basin of water which caught Wang Xin before he could jump out of the way. She quickly slammed the door close.

"Who was that?" Wang Xin asked.

The boatman replied: "Ge Xiaoda's sister and Xiugu's sister-in-law."

Wang again thought to himself: "She could be an important witness but she is not recorded in the files." He knocked at the door and two black eyes peeped through a crack.

"Has your family any silk floss for sale?" Wang Xin asked.

"No," said the child.

He made haste to say: "You've splashed me all over. Could you wipe it off for me?"

She opened the door and let him in.

The room was disorderly and she picked up a rag from her sewing basket and gave it to Wang Xin.

As he wiped his clothes, he caught sigh of a gold watch in the basket and wondered how they could afford such a valuable watch. He opened it and saw an inscription: "Zihe".

"Since you have no silk floss, will you sell me this watch?" he said.

He produced twenty silver dollars and Sangu's eyes sparkled with astonishment.

As soon as he came out of the house he told the boatman that he was returning to Hangzhou.

Ah Yi commented: "Why in such a hurry? Anybody would think that you were the commissioner himself."

Wang Xin asked if he knew anyone by the name of Zihe but as he did not know the surname, the boatman was unable to help.

As the boat sailed on there came an order from an official boat lying at anchor ordering them not to draw near. Wang Xin told Ah Yi to ignore the order and row over.

The guards on the boat raised their rifles and shouted: "Are you looking for death?"

A rifle went off and the boatman screamed with terror as poles reached down and hooked onto the boat.

A soldier raised a rattan stick to strike Ah Yi but Wang Xin in a voice of authority ordered him to stop. An officer then appeared and, recognizing his master, instantly went down on his knees before Wang Xin. "Forgive us, Your Excellency," he said.

Wang Xin helped the boatman up and apologized for fooling him, but Ah Yi knelt before him and begged him to solve Yang Naiwu's case.

Taking the Prisoners to the Capital

WHEN Wang Xin walked into the cabin he saw a desk full of name cards and gifts covered by red cloth. He lifted the cloth and saw gold, sparkling pearls and silver ingots. A clerk gave him a list which named all the officials who had presented the gifts and who had also handled Yang Naiwu's case. The list was headed by provincial governor Yang Changjun, who had given twenty thousand; the Judicial Commissioner Kuai Hesun — fifteen thousand; provincial Literary Chancellor Hu Ruilan — fifteen thousand and Prefect Chen Lu — fifteen thousand. There were many other names, and not wanting to read on Wang asked: "How much does it all amount to?"

"Altogether a hundred thousand taels," answered the clerk.

What should he do, thought Wang. If he rejected the money, the officials would be nervous and perhaps kill the prisoners and remove a few sheets of the files. He had boasted he would bring both to the capital intact. He decided he would have to accept the money and thus lull their suspicions.

"Accept the lot," he instructed the surprised clerk.

The clerk wrote letters of thanks and signed the commissioner's name. On receiving the acknowledgement, the officials felt a great weight had been lifted off them.

Both Naiwu and Xiugu were taken to the commissioner's lodge.

A glimmer of hope rose in Naiwu when he saw the official notices placed against the hall wall. On one was written "The Eminent Censor," and the other "The Commissioner". He knew his sister must have been successful in the capital and the commissioner had come to collect the prisoners. He looked up to the upturned eaves of the hall and saw an eagle flying in a blue sky studded with white clouds.

Naiwu had decided to plead innocence even if it meant he would be tortured to death. At least he would leave an unsolved case for posterity.

Among the witnesses was little Sangu who immediately ran over to Xiugu and gave her a hug.

Other witnesses were Ge Wenqing, and Qian Baosheng ... Liu Xitong, the first interrogator, stood to the side.

To the beating of drums and gongs, Wang Xin entered, dressed in official gown and cap, and sat down. The provincial judge handed him a list of the prisoners' names and a list of the files which were kept in a sealed chest and asked him to check them.

Wang Xin ordered the escort to take good care of the prisoners and promised them ten dollars for every pound the prisoners gained on the way to Beijing.

"If they gain ten pounds," he said, "you'll get 100 dollars."

The escort could not believe their luck, but their elation was soon dashed when Wang Xin's next sentence was: "If they lose a pound you'll be flogged a hundred times. And if they lose five pounds you'll get three years' hard labour, and if ten pounds, exiled, and if they die...," Wang Xin hissed, "you'll pay with your lives."

Wang Xin ordered that Naiwu and Xiugu be weighed and then to prevent them from committing suicide by using their hair to hang themselves, he ordered that their plaits be dipped in paint and coiled on top of their heads.

A fleet of boats set off. The prisoners aboard were closely watched by soldiers. Liu Xitong was looking at a small boat at the end of the fleet where his wife and son were. He had lost all his former airs and his wife and son were making haste to arrive at the capital before the commissioner to seek out connections and buy themselves out of trouble. His concubine had other plans and had accompanied him.

When night came and all were asleep, the concubine got up, wrapped her jewellery box with a kerchief and tiptoed out of the cabin and made her way towards a big tree. Someone jumped out from behind it. "Shhh!" he whispered. It was Secretary Zhao of the Yuhang County *yamen*. "Did you bring everything?"

She patted the jewellery box.

"The old man will be finished when Yang Naiwu is cleared," he said, "and you and I will be involved too. Let's go."

They moved over to a small paddle-boat but black clouds began to gather and a strong wind blew. Secretary Zhao ordered the boatman to set off for Shaoxing but he said the wind was too strong. Zhao produced ten silver dollars and the boatman untied the boat and began rowing.

The storm blew stronger, tossing the boat like a toy. A towering wave suddenly engulfed it. The concubine popped her head up once above the waves and then disappeared. All that was left of the secretary was his cap which bobbed on top of the water.

Lin Ziyi, although a sixth grade assistant in the Board of Punishments, was as poor as a church mouse. He was the adopted son of Liu Xitong, and the family called on him as soon as they arrived in the capital.

Lin was not very welcoming but Mrs. Liu, her face wreathed in smiles, asked how they were.

Lin's wife said: "We're too poor to feel fine," and they asked if Mrs. Liu had come to buy another post for her husband as she had done in the past.

"Oh, forget him," she cried. "It's all this one's fault, the little beast..." she pointed to her son.

Liu Zihe hung his head.

Only rich people help the poor, not vice versa. But since Lin worked in the Board of Punishments, he was asked to help. This was another example of "The person in charge can do more than a real official."

Mrs. Liu presented them with a case filled with silver ingots.

With water underneath, a boat moves. When in dire straits, money buys lives.

Mrs. Lin clasped the case and cried with pleasure.

Lin asked how much was in the case and Mrs. Liu answered: "A thousand taels."

Lin said he needed two thousand taels to bribe the heads and court runners in the *yamen*. Lin thought for a moment and then added: "We will pretend to torture Little Cabbage. If she doesn't feel any pain, she won't confess. We'll use the same method on all except Yang Naiwu."

Liu Zihe exclaimed: "Wonderful. The one in charge can really do more than the official."

Meanwhile, Wang Xin had arrived in Beijing with the prisoners and witnesses. Together with Prince Chun, Sang Chunrong and Xia Tongshan, he discussed the best way to search out the truth.

Sang, the minister of the Board of Punishments, said to Wang Xin: "Thanks to your wit and intelligence, you've brought them all here in one piece and not a single sheet of the files is missing."

"Incorrect," said Xia. "They have one witness too many. That is Sangu."

They all laughed and Prince Chun took a pinch of snuff, sneezed a few times and in high spirits asked Sang: "How are you going to conduct the proceedings tomorrow?"

Sang said he would have to preside over the interrogation together with the infantry commandant, the vice-minister of the court of censors and the Grand Councillor Bao Jun."

Prince Chun was displeased because Bao Jun was the trusted follower of Prince Gong, the sixth son of Emperor Daoguang, while Prince Chun was the seventh son. The brothers had their own followers and vied with each other. But Sang said it was on the orders of the Empress Dowager herself.

That night, at the residence of the grand chancellor, the reception hall was ablaze with candlelight.

Liu Xitong, like a cat on a hot tin roof, sat waiting for his return and as soon as the chancellor came in, he hurried over. Without going through the formal greetings, Bao Jun asked him what he had done to be so much trouble. Liu Xitong began: "We've been long-standing friends…"

Bao Jun rudely cut him short: "Under the imperial decree the interrogation tomorrow will be presided over by three officials. I can't do what I like. Besides, if people knew you have called on me so late at night…." He was sending Liu packing.

Liu Xitong said quickly: "I have brought a letter from the provincial governor, judge and treasurer of Zhejiang and some presents."

Bao Jun glanced casually at the gifts. "I know the hardships provincial officials have to go through. If this case is reversed, not only the hundred or so officials in Zhejiang will lose their posts, you might even lose your life…."

Liu Xitong went down on his knees. "Please save us, Your Excellency, for old times' sake." Bao Jun promised to do his best. Liu knocked his head again and again on the floor.

With the three high officials presiding, the courtroom of the Board of Punishments had an oppressive air.

By the sides of the room were the insignia placards of the grand councillor, the minister of the Board of Punishments, the infantry commandant and the senior vice-minister of the court of censors.

At a long table placed in the middle sat Grand Councillor Bao Jun and the minister of the Board of Punishments Sang Chunrong and on the right the infantry commandant and on the left the senior vice-minister. Clerks and court runners stood around the court room.

In a side chamber Prince Chun sat on a fur-lined couch with Wang Xin and Xia Tongshan on either side of him where they could watch the proceedings going on in the courtroom.

Sang leaned over to Bao and asked which prisoner they should interrogate first.

Bao suggested Xiugu because he was afraid that if they started on Naiwu first he would cause too much trouble. A shaking Xiugu was brought in.

"Take a look around," ordered Sang.

She saw the four imposing officials, the ferocious court runners waiting to pounce like eagles. Nearby were torture instruments.

Sang said: "The court of the Board of Punishments enforces the law strictly and does not bend it for the benefit of friends and relatives. Now tell the truth. Did Yang Naiwu kill your husband?"

She shook her head.

"Did the two of you commit adultery and then murder?"

She shook her head again.

"Who was your lover then?"

Xiugu hesitated. "There was no adulterer," she said.

Sang ordered the torture instruments to be brought.

The night before, the chained Xiugu was curled up in the corner of a dimly lit cell. The door opened and a hoarse voice announced: "I'm here to inspect the prison." The head goaler entered followed by another one.

The second goaler grasped Xiugu's wrist and addressed her in a soft voice. It was Liu Zihe who, pretending to be concerned, told her he had given bribes to all around in the Board of Punishments so that they would only pretend to torture her.

"You have fed me enough lies," Xiugu cried out in anger.

Liu Zihe insisted it was because he loved her and urged her to stick to her original confession and not admit to Naiwu's innocence. "Money buys lives when necessary," he said, "and all crows are black, as the saying goes. When you realize that there will be no pain when you are 'tortured' you'll know I am not cheating you."

The crusher was placed on Xiugu's fingers and the order given to pull.

To Xiugu's surprise what Liu Zihe had said was true, she felt no pain and again she heard his words: "Money buys lives when necessary and all crows are black."

She finally realized the ability of people like Liu Zihe who could even bribe the whole *yamen* of the Board of Punishments and that Naiwu's life and hers could never be saved.

The torturers were anxious when Xiugu did not pretend to feel pain so they trod on her foot in order to make her cry out.

This did not escape the eyes of Sang, the minister of the Board of Punishments, and with great interest Prince Chun watched from the side.

Now the torturers placed the finger crusher on Sangu's fingers.

Sang asked her first: "Who is your sister-in-law's adulterer?"

Sangu said she did not know and the order was given to use the finger crusher.

Sangu pretended to cry out in pain.

She was asked: "Do your fingers hurt?"

"Not at all," said the naive Sangu.

Everyone was shocked to see such a brazen violation of the law at the Board of Punishments and all eyes turned to the minister of the Board of Punishments.

He pretended nothing untoward had taken place and ordered Yang Naiwu to be brought in.

Barely had he knelt down, Naiwu cried out: "I am innocent."

Sang pulled out his confession. "Didn't you put your signature on this confession?"

Naiwu told him to look carefully at the signature.

When Sang examined it, the signature read: "Forced confession."

Naiwu had written in the style of calligraphy used in cutting seals.

Liu Xitong was asked if he had used torture on Naiwu to get the confession.

"A little," he admitted.

At the word "little" Naiwu tore his clothes off and showed the scars and wounds made by the torture instruments. Prince Chun at the side exploded in anger: "This Yuhang magistrate is too outrageous."

Liu Xitong tried to shed his responsibility by saying that Naiwu had used bad language and that he always treated gentlemen with reason and by the law but he had been forced to use torture.

Naiwu burst out: "You are the lowest of the low."

Liu commented: "You see, Your Excellency, how he ignores the presence of you four high officials and calls names at the official appointed by the imperial court?"

Bao Jun said: "I think Yang Naiwu is a vicious man. He has had nine bearings and nine times he has been sentenced. If his case is overturned by the Board of Punishments, no one will want to be a provincial official anymore."

Yang Naiwu was overcome with indignation: "I thought the law was enforced in the court of the Board of Punishments and never expected that even here, officials cover up for each other."

Sang pounded the table with his gavel: "It is apparent that you committed adultery and murder. Yet you forced your sister to file a petition at the Board of Punishments. Tonight you can have a good meal and be executed tomorrow!" The pronouncement was so sudden that the infantry commandant and the censor looked at each other in consternation and Prince Chun jumped up with fury, cursing out loud.

Sitting beside Sang, Bao Jun, the grand councillor, nodded his head slightly. He was satisfied.

To be sentenced to death so quickly made Naiwu shriek out: "I have not been asked to make a confession yet!" But Sang overruled him, saying that the Board required no such confession and turning to Liu Xitong he said kindly: "I'll report to the emperor and have the two beheaded tomorrow. You can return to Yuhang."

Liu Xitong kowtowed in relief.

The audience dispersed and Sang went into the sideroom where Prince Chun demanded how much the magistrate had bribed him and grabbed him to the Empress Dowager.

But Sang whispered to him: "I'm arranging a secret meeting tonight for Yang Naiwu and Xiugu, at which I shall be eavesdropping."

The prince was baffled but Wang Xin and Xia knew

the true intention and eventually the prince admitted that even the grand councillor had been taken in by the court proceedings.

"This is more thrilling than any opera," he said, "I shall definitely be listening in as well."

Lifelong Affinity

AT the back of the *yamen* of the Board of Punishments was a row of three exquisitely furnished rooms with a corridor running along the front and trees and flowers on either side of the row. This was Sang Chunrong's private quarters where he often worked.

That evening a table was laid with food and wine and two red candles were lit. A gaoler brought in Yang Naiwu to eat his last meal before execution. There were two pairs of chopsticks on the table and he wondered who was going to eat with him.

"I'll find some company for you," said the gaoler as he walked out of the room.

Naiwu sat down and as he picked up his chopsticks and pot of wine he thought: "Could it be her to keep me company?" His heart filled with warmth.

With lantern in hand, the gaoler led Xiugu into a moon-shaped door leading to the corridor outside the door of the room. As she entered their eyes met and she turned and ran out but the gaoler blocked her way and said: "His Excellency ordered us to give you two a good meal before you die."

Yang Naiwu walked to meet her, his emotions in a state of confusion. But he controlled himself, held his hands out and called to her sarcastically: "Don't you know that it is the custom of the Qing Dynasty that two adulterers can meet and talk on the night before their execution? Do come in, Mrs. Ge."

Xiugu felt too ashamed to face him, but as if reading her thoughts, he said: "Tonight we will only talk about how we were wronged," and then in a kinder voice said: "It's too windy out here, Xiugu, come inside."

As the door was closed, Xiugu was gripped by panic. "What shall I say if he asks me who my seducer was?"

Instead, Naiwu urged her to come and eat. Her silence angered him and he pounded the table exclaiming: "This is really outrageous! Here I am begging you to eat before my execution and you refuse to budge. Do I owe you anything?"

Xiugu hastened toward him and knelt down and wept. Naiwu helped her up and filled a cup of wine. "We are here together in this room tonight, thousands of miles away from home. Tomorrow our heads will be severed from our bodies. We will meet again in the nether world. Come, let's drink. A great man does not rejoice for living and is not saddened when dying. Without birth, there is no death, without death no birth. Birth and death; death and birth. I've seen everything."

Xiugu gazed at Naiwu. Could this be the handsome and charming Mr. Yang, this man with paint stuck on top of his head and his face stubbly and haggard?

"I can't drink," she said sorrowfully.

"But we're celebrating," Naiwu said. "Although we were not born at the same time on the same day as lovers should, we will be dying tomorrow. I don't mind dying for you but not falsely accused as an adulterer. Even in death I shall not know who the real adulterer is and why I should die. That is the tragedy."

Xiugu spoke: "Master Yang, I have repaid your kindness by bringing calamity on your whole family. Kill me now. I want to die before you." She threw herself down.

He helped her up. "I would be resigned to the fact that all my property has gone on this lawsuit and my reputation ruined but my poor sister has suffered dreadfully. When I am beheaded tomorrow, she will be found guilty of lodging a false complaint. She will not escape execution either."

Xiugu threw herself into his arms. "I am full of regrets," she said. "For having met you and involving you. Now it's too late. You were framed! Liu Zihe was my seducer!"

Suddenly the doors of the side rooms opened and Prince Chun, Sang Chunrong, Wang Xin and Xia Tongshan walked in.

"Good," said the prince triumphantly.

Both Naiwu and Xiugu were flabbergasted.

At last the case of the two which had lasted three years was coming to an end. Sang Chunrong, minister of the Board of Punishments, announced solemnly in court: "Liu Zihe, son of the magistrate of Yuhang, committed the crime of killing the husband in order to get the wife. He is sentenced to death and is to be beheaded immediately!" Qiang Baosheng is guilty of supplying arsenic to commit the murder and also to be beheaded immediately." The two men, screaming in fear, were taken away by the executioners.

Sang continued: "Liu Xitong, magistrate of Yuhang County, tried to cover up his son's crime and pin it on a person he harboured a grudge against. He is to be removed from office and exiled to the northeast border. He will not qualify for an amnesty."

Liu Xitong was stripped of his official gown and cap with the button denoting his rank.

Sang continued: "Yang Naiwu, although framed and ill-treated, brought this on himself by teaching Xiugu how to read Buddhist sutras and write instead of keeping his distance from her. His title of provincial graduate will not be restored. He will be given fifty feet of white cloth as compensation and sent home to plant fields and occupy his time by reading." Naiwu kowtowed and accepted the white cloth, saddened at the outcome of three years' suffering.

Prince Chun asked Wang Xin: "Yang Naiwu was an innocent victim, why hasn't his title been restored?"

Wang Xin answered: "He is the cause of over a hundred Qing officials being demoted."

Sang went on with his verdicts: "Xiugu, for not keeping her distance from Yang Naiwu, has not behaved in the manner of proper womanly behaviour. She falsely accused Yang Naiwu, but taking into account that she had been forced, leniency has been shown. She will be hanged instead of beheaded."

Prince Chun asked: "Why must Little Cabbage be hanged?"

Wang Xin answered: "That is the law."

Xiugu was satisfied that her head would not be removed from her body. She bowed and thanked the minister.

A eunuch galloped into the *yamen* and jumping off his horse cried: "A decree from the Old Buddha. Xiugu is to be taken to the palace!"

In the Palace of Eternal Spring, the Empress Dowager sat on a couch carved with a dragon and phoenix motif. She was curious to see the famous Little Cabbage, whether she was as beautiful as described. At the same time, she knew that she would be praised by her ministers for showing kindness to the unfortunate young woman. Xiugu was awed by the splendour of the palace and knew nothing about court etiquette. She went on bowing repeatedly until the anxious eunuch spoke for her: "Xiugu presents herself to the Old Buddha."

The Empress Dowager was impressed by the beautiful woman before her. "How old are you?" she asked.

"I am twenty-three," answered Xiugu.

"And you've been in prison for three years?"

The chief eunuch, seeing that the Empress Dowager was impressed with Xiugu, piped up:

"How pitiable. She's so young."

When the Empress Dowager heard that Xiugu was to be hanged, the eunuch said: "A country girl would of course succumb under pressure and confess to anything."

Xiugu was asked to hold out her hands, and the Empress Dowager wrote on her palms with a brush: "Overlook her crime and send her back home."

Xiugu gasped and the eunuch quickly spoke up for her: "Thank the Old Buddha for her benevolence."

When the Empress Dowager heard that Xiugu had no family and admitted she still had feelings for Naiwu, she suggested that she should stay with him and care for him in order to repay the wrong she had done.

But Xiugu said: "That won't do. If I should marry him, people would believe that we really had had an affair. That would be bad for his reputation. Besides, I am too ashamed to face his family."

The Empress Dowager nodded her agreement and her face fell as she noticed the button on the hat of the chief eunuch. She realized that over a hundred officials were involved in this case. So she said: "You have sinned and caused the demotion of over a hundred of my officials. Go to a nunnery and repent so that you'll have a good life in your next one."

Xiugu remembered what her mother-in-law had told her: "Women have come to this world to suffer."

She prostrated herself before the Empress Dowager, forgetting to give her thanks for her benevolence.

Xiugu was taken back to the Board of Punishments and raised the palms of her hands to show the decree written by the Empress Dowager.

In the *yamen* of the governor of Zhejiang Province, Wang Xin stood in the main hall with the imperial decree in his hands.

The buttons of rank and plumes on the hats of the provincial governor, judge and treasurer were removed as were those of all the other officials who had handled the Yang Naiwu case.

The prefect of Hangzhou, Chen Lu, hung a piece of white silk from a beam and thought of suicide.

Meanwhile the container was filling up with red, blue and crystal buttons of office as one by one they were removed.

Epilogue

ANOTHER spring had arrived. The scenery of Yuhang remained the same. The water flowed under the Stone Lion Bridge. The two pagodas, one male and one female, stood on Pagoda Hill.

But spring did not come to Yang Naiwu and Little Cabbage.

He had survived the ordeal, but all his property was gone, his title removed. He had no income and planted mulberry trees and raised silkworms for a living. He was dressed like a labourer and had a slight limp as he entered his home with a basket of mulberry leaves. He now lived in a two-storey house in a narrow lane. Tired, he sat at his desk, dull-eyed as he thought of his old study where he had written a poem before a white porcelain statue of Boddhisattava while Xiugu sang to the accompaniment of a fiddle:

> *"A rare beauty as you are*
> *Ought not to have fallen into the dusty world.*
> *Forced into a liaison, we are destined for each other.*
> *Our ties will last like the ever-rolling waters."*

Overcome with the memory he picked up his brush:

> *"The Jin and the Wei Rivers should never meet,*
> *Since ancient times, right should be differentiated from wrong.*

*Close your mind to the past
And sit meekly on a hassock under the azure clouds."*

Naiwu limped along a narrow path outside the south city gate and headed for the nunnery where the door opened and Sangu emerged wiping away her tears. She did not recognize Naiwu, so he slowly walked into the nunnery where the drumming of a wooden fish was heard and smoke rose from the incense sticks and candles. He saw her, Xiugu, whose head shaved as a nun, sitting on a hassock with her eyes closed and her palms together reciting sutras. His heart gave a pang as he backed away and closed the door.

He looked up at the blue sky and white clouds, the sound of the wooden fish pounding his ears. He pulled out the poem he had written for her, tore it into pieces and tossed them into the air as if he was tossing away the injustice of the world, his anger and sadness. The pieces fluttered in the wind and he recited to himself:

*"The Jin and the Wei Rivers should never meet,
Since ancient times, right should be differentiated from wrong.
Close your mind to the past
And sit meekly on a hassock under the azure clouds."*

He walked away as evening drew near, the falling leaves and torn paper becoming smaller and smaller in the distance.

图书在版编目（CIP）数据

杨乃武与小白菜：英文/ 方艾著.—北京：中国文学出版社，1994.7

ISBN 7-5071-0224-6/I.221（外）

I.杨… II.方… III.① 小说－中国－现代－英文 IV.I247.8

杨乃武与小白菜

方 艾

熊猫丛书

*

中国文学出版社出版
（中国北京百万庄路24号）
中国国际图书贸易总公司发行
（中国北京车公庄西路 35号）
北京邮政信箱第399号　邮政编码100044
1994年 第1版（英）
ISBN 7-5071-0224-6/I.221
01500
10-E-2907P